[mercury under my tongue]

[mercury under my tongue]

[mercury under my tongue]

SYLVAIN TRUDEL

■

TRANSLATED BY SHEILA FISCHMAN

SOFTSKULL
BROOKLYN, NY

1-933368-96-9

The translation of Mercury Under my Tongue is made possible by a grant from

Library of Congress Cataloging-in-Publication Data

Trudel, Sylvain, 1963–
  [Du mercure sous la langue. English]
  Mercury under my tongue / by Sylvain Trudel ; translated by Sheila Fischman.
      p. cm.
  ISBN-13: 978-1-933368-96-2
  ISBN-10: 1-933368-96-9
  I. Fischman, Sheila. II. Title.

PQ3919.2.T79D813 2008
843'.914--dc22
                                    2007028511

Cover design by Luke Gerwe
Interior design by Pauline Neuwirth, Neuwirth & Associates
Printed in the United States of America

Soft Skull Press
An Imprint of Counterpoint LLC
2117 Fourth St
Berkeley CA 94710

www.softskull.com
www.counterpointpress.com

Distributed by Publishers Group West

10 9 8 7 6 5 4 3 2 1

Butterflies drown
in this stream
as my heart falls,
and now my heart cries
and now it follows
the course of the running water,
icy water,
eager to run to its death,
that carries away with the leaves,
all hope of rejuvenation.

MARILOU D., AGE 15

INTELLIGENCE IS ALL well and good, but if you want to unstick your eyelids first thing in the morning you need to forget everything you know. When I'm in bad shape I practically feel I should apologize for knowing so much about so many things, for not believing kind and reassuring words, for feeling vermin crawl under the pats on the back, but it's not my fault: I've been an atheist since birth, and the holy water of baptism didn't cleanse my wicked soul and anyway, both my neck and my knees have always been stiff. I'm what they call an asshole, a know-it-all, a mall-rat rebel, a useless little bugger, who doesn't like anything. But at least, living my life like a snail, all curled up inside myself, I don't bite anyone; and basically, I'm not that bad. Outside myself, I can see that people now live surrounded by the sorrow of things; it's very different from the time when romantics used to cherish death, because nowadays we don't like to die. You want proof? Nowadays people blow their brains out, hang themselves in the cellar, slash their wrists, drink poison, or jump into a river or in front of a train. That's not dying, that's terminating life, stopping it once and for all; that's not sticking around. We no longer play with fire, but we do put an end to our suffering, which is not the same thing. We no longer whine the way we used to because we no longer have any hope of one day being understood. Being a romantic to the tips of your eyelashes means dissolving into tears at the drop of a hat, over trivial matters; and you have to philosophize about the cruelty of the world and the horrors of the centuries. To enjoy dying, you have to devote yourself to a sensitive public that's drunk on passion, but when romantics offer you their heart like that, they turn your stomach. Luckily, those days are over and done with and that's that. Nowadays unhappy people are alone with their despair. We live in a golden age of isolation and of harsh truth that we can no longer tolerate or share. Icy cold is good for humans: it's healthy, but at the same time it cuts away so much that it dehumanizes. That's the real world though, and it's neither good nor bad, neither fish nor fowl, merely the world as it's reflected in the shiny little shoes of those who are condemned to live; and it means that no one is in love with martyrdom any more, the only martyrs now are martyrs to love.

And that's it, I'm ready to roll: this is a good day. That's how I see it and it's no lie. So I talk on and on, yadayadayada till I get on my own nerves, because the mysteries of the universe are so vast that I feel kind of pathetic for having an opinion on the matter, but I beg my own pardon: I'm a dream that is coming unraveled and there won't be a sequel, that's what defeats me. This sour thought makes for a painful waking, but it leads to a healthy life for anyone who can get up on his own. Oh, I don't feel much yet what's happening to me is too intense, I have a kind of dark faith in myself, but waiting doesn't cost me anything, no, I wait for free, room and board, that's the gift life is offering me, and once the disease appears in broad daylight, skimming the skin and brushing the bones, I'll want to tear away the last remaining flesh, as it is written. My poor feet have always picked up any disease that's going around, until whatever is going around is the worst one possible and I jump into it with both feet; what happens next is logical, I suppose, maybe even normal, but it's a shame to end up like that, I mean without having really begun, without having succeeded at anything that's too fine. A person feels a little mean because he has taken everything and given nothing back, which leaves a bitter taste in the dice cup; yet all hopes were permitted and all the elements brought together as planets around my sun: I had a mother, a father, and grandparents, with a brother and sister thrown in for good measure, a dog—the works; and I also had friends, true friends, good friends, the kind that don't drop you when there's a hint of a cloud. Alas, I can't deny it: it was all for nothing.

Had I known, I'd have given myself a more powerful kick in the ass, I'd have started to live before today, but now it's too late and my life will have been without qualities, without richness: I was born with holes in my hands, like crucified remains. But the worst thing is that in the end it's not cowardice that kills; the worst thing is that a living death can last for a very long time; and that the Grim Reaper kills a walking corpse—a baker's dozen is the rate among the wicked. Goddammit to fucking hell! Whoops, it's true: blasphemy isn't nice, it makes the icons weep; but it just came out by itself and when it came out it brought out the wicked too. That's because, on my own, I'm a little ossuary at the bottom of the barrel. Had I, while still in my mother's womb, helped an old lady cross the street, I could have told myself: "Ah yes, I deserve to live, it's my reward." But I've never done any good deed to deserve life and now I deserve to have it taken away from me—it's geometrical.

> *To turn back*
> *the river of time*
> *is an inhuman task;*
> *might as well try to find*
> *saffron on the moon.*

Slowly I close my eyes that are boiling with fever and I don't really know what it is that I see, but it's better than when I open them and that says it all. There are undulating forms that resemble shape shifters; phosphorescent mysteries that want to teach me ageless secrets or some strange philosophy; and there are times when it's so beautiful that I think I'm already dead. Sometimes faces that I've loved come to repopulate my solitude. It's as though they've burst out of an Aladdin's lamp, smiling and gracious like good genies, but when I want to hold them close to me, I wrap my arms around nothingness.

It's wild, but I never would have thought that I'd arrive so soon at the world's farthest extremity, where the slightest glance from me would scratch this fragile universe of crystal that no longer understands me. To some extent I'm already elsewhere, spat out far away from the simple things that make up everyday life, with one foot in the molasses of the nights. Armchair psychologists or front-porch philosophers who watch too much TV talk about stages or phases. Which come before the end, if I understand what I mean.

Last year on August 6, I was six thousand days old, and now I'm rich with the dreams of more than six thousand nights but poor from the same number of wakenings. Soon, very soon, I will live my final night, my final morning, my final hour, I'll expel my final breath between my teeth. But it's strange, I feel as if I'm talking about someone else, a total stranger with no face and no emotions. When I think that as a snot-nosed brat I used to wonder seriously when "soon" was and if "somewhere" was far away, I practically feel like bawling.

> *Somewhere,*
> *is anywhere at all,*
> *between the tip of a nose and the end of the world;*
> *and soon,*
> *is any time at all,*
> *between now and the night.*

It's funny but it's also not funny: men are crucified like slaves on their own pain, aware of tragedy but at the same time terrified of themselves, with one eye a coward's yellow and the other a murderer's black, and they look in opposite directions in the same devious face, but the men aren't too sure what they are or where they're going and that kills me, seeing that I've only ever asked the stars for one thing: to have some idea of where I would go and what I would do, so that I won't die unhappy and despondent. But I'll have messed up everything, both my exit and my entrance. A friend who's recovering from meningitis read my Egyptian tarot cards on her hospital table this morning, under meaningful looks from the nurses, and at the crucial moment I drew the Sword of Tears. Which does not bode well. And this fall, the onions have thick skins: it's going to be a hard winter.

It's odd, but the Egyptian tarot reminded me of the back lanes in the parish of Sainte-Philomène on Sundays when we used to play at reading the future in the entrails of pigeons sprayed with gunshot: we were idiots, we thought that the world would always be the world and that we ourselves would always be the same. We thought we'd live forever without trying to with no clouds on the horizon to cast a shadow over the picture. All that, we read in the lobes of the liver, in the folds of the crop in the gullet, and we took away hallucinations in our own birdbrains. We were such idiots that I still carry some shame within me, a hatred of what we were.

> *I wanted to leave you*
> *a message*
> *on the mirror of your night*
> *or to play for you ad infinitum*
> *a little music,*
> *like a whispering love,*
> *but I'm a small unreadable book*
> *its pages stuck together*
> *like the wings*
> *of dried butterflies.*

Mama, sometimes I smell the honey of your warm breath as it flows down my shivering neck; I hear your heart beating under your red nails, your nails bitten into little cockscombs at the tips of your mustard fingers, your clenched, smoker's fingers; I think about the polished stars left swirling in your wake; and inwardly I smile. You made the smile that I carry and you gave it a name, my true hidden name, I mean, not my official one. I'd like to talk about my secret name that no one knows except you and me, a name that's as deep as a wound because of the pain of being one-self and nothing better, my eternal name that's murmured in the night, the burn on the heart from my baptism of fire.

Mama, I remember that you didn't say very much because you were listening to the radio where sad women talked about their woes, but I didn't give a damn about our silences. We conversed in other ways, with our eyes, like deaf-mutes, but it was no worse. I loved you purely in the kitchen of my childhood, and you still shine in me like an inner cosmos; you are another starry sky that opens onto the infinite within, while I am the constriction between those two eternities; I am the pang of anguish through which the frightened blood of every human must flow one day, where everything must live or die, and I wish I could have lived just to please you, to make you laugh, to live until you died with your hand in mine, and then to die myself, in your still warm footprints, in your perfume that will have been my own, now melted into air, into thin air, and surrounded by your objects that I love as if they were alive.

Ah! Mama, my poisoned blood hisses and pounds at my head and I want to cry and kill myself, but that would kill you from anxiety or sorrow, so I punch my throat with my fist and wait for it to pass, or for it to come, finally, once and for all.

Mama, as long as my heart goes on beating, my eyes go on seeing, as long as my consciousness knows, I won't allow a single fearful, feeble lament to escape my lips, cross my heart.

> *The key to the nights*
> *lies at the bottom of the sea*
> *where it dreams that it has been*
> *a silent mouth,*
> *and my drowning is a dream*
> *where all my wishes gleam*
> *like open wounds,*
> *where I find at last the key to the nights,*
> *all the voices of a lifetime,*
> *all the faces of a day on Earth.*

To my great misfortune, I have never believed in anything as simple as cloudless happiness, because I believe that things are at the same time good and bad, true or false depending on the day, sometimes even according to the varied nature of the light on a single day; anyway, things are often so murky that you see yourself as lost in the world, you think we're going to die because of all the things you no longer understand, as if you knew you were on the brink of noth-ingness, a toe's width from the fatal fall, and I sense that our souls can die as surely as our bodies. To put it another way, we die on all sides all at once and at every moment, and that knowledge eats quietly away at our bones and brains, with a sound like the gnawing of a rat, until the day of the final sigh, when the rotten heart bursts. Many times I would like to speed it up, to be racing to my ruin like a madman, but there's a problem: I'm afraid that I'm too big a coward to put an end to my ordeal on my own; barehanded. But the opposite could also be true: maybe I'm so strong that for me, the horror of pain and suffering is child's play compared with the horror of annihilation and of everlasting solitude.

Oh, I don't understand anything any more and my head is throbbing with pain and now I don't even want to understand the things that threaten me, because I'll never be able to trounce them, but those things bite into me so hard that they throttle me, it's all right though, it's all right, I unbutton my pajamas and breathe through my nose.

It's nothing, nothing serious, I'm just having a bad day, the kind that are so numerous in the life of a man, even a young man.

Sorrow sits
at the foot of my bed,
pretending to read

a newspaper with a story about
a fire in a church.

Papa, you scare me when your eyes switch off in a breath of anguish. You have always talked to me through secret signs, with your hands, your face, your breathing, and I've always understood whatever you meant by your sighs and tics; I know the hidden meaning of all your awkward acts as if I'd knitted you. With me, you don't have a hope of hiding inside some role: I hold onto you by every corner of the veil that lets me see you all the way into invisibility, to a place where you may not even know yourself.

When the bells ring out on the grey roofs of Sainte-Philomène parish, I'll take along in my pockets some enduring images of you: a tired man in an undershirt, slumped on the living room sofa at the end of the day, his face spattered by the blue chill of the TV screen; a grouchy man who scrapes his face with dull razorblades in the morning, who is bored on Sunday and spends his time in the refrigerator, who sucks milk straight from the carton; a poor man who smokes his pack a day and spits his lungs into the sink; a paranoid man certain that everyone on the street is judging him; a husband who's embarrassed to kiss his wife in front of his children. But above all, it's your soul that I will take with me when I go, your soul which is in a state of nervous tension that makes your two left hands tremble; but a man's hands are his magical children who never get old, his little palm-readers who always peddle truth to the left and right: did you know that? Unlike me, for whom lying is like breathing and who slams into a wall at a hundred miles an hour. Today, on the other hand, I can see that you could also die; I sense you strangled, bleeding to death, and I know that I'm the one who worries you; don't be afraid though, Papa, I'll work things out just fine on my own; and anyway I'm not the first, don't be so dramatic. It's true: this has been going on for millions of years and it works perfectly well, so well that it's not going to stop tomorrow; billions of sleepwalkers have already lost their footing and taken a tumble and fallen off the Earth, and it means practically nothing now, if you think about it. If I were the first one to fall, it might be different, but on a cosmic scale it's insignificant; anyway, oblivion can't hurt any more than everyday life and I'm not afraid. Whatever happens, in due course someone will help me cross the River Lethe, some ghost or angel or soul, some kind of Saint Christopher, or a great winged white horse, something, or maybe Grandpa Langlois. But poor you, look at yourself: you're as pale as the moon and you're worried sick. So button up your overcoat, Papa, and take a walk around the block, buy yourself a case of beer, some smokes, and a lottery ticket at the grocery store. It will do you good to surrender yourself to a fate different from mine; and a fair wind will put some color in your cheeks.

Verily I say unto you, I told you the truth: I've always believed in you and I've always tried to find your light deep inside the closets, sought your warmth all the way to the sagging mattress of your bed, thinking that you are everywhere and nowhere, like a holy ghost, and I was not mistaken: when I talk to you I feel as if I'm praying to God; you're so remote and unreal, you seem so unattainable; but snap out of it, Papa, please; I'm afraid you'll always be a slave to the fear you were born with, fear that's now suffocating you, fear that is your wheat, your daily bread, your poor man's communion wafer.

As you can see, Papa dear, I have a penchant for the apocalyptic and I like to think of myself as a biblical prophet—have you noticed? From the depths of my small stature it makes me look as if I look down on everything from the peak of my great height, where I play the copper rooster atop a church steeple, but from which alas I see nothing good, neither rain nor fine weather, neither the best days hidden by snow and storm nor the one swallow that would finally make this spring that I've been waiting for forever, not even a hint of the morning of our reconciliation, or of my so longed-for impossible cure.

Yes, Papa, life is as simple as hello and as complicated as a farewell, but in the secrecy of my silence and the silence of my secret, I love your feverish, abnormal soul.

> *I hate the day,*
> *that rain of insults*
> *where I began to rot*
> *in the belly of things,*
> *and I hate the night,*
> *that bitch made pregnant by another man,*
> *who sweeps a poor wretch away*
> *to deep within her flower.*

In our civilized lands, people prefer to die from the heart: it's more noble than dying from the bladder, guts, or balls. It's cleaner than cirrhosis or a hemorrhage, it looks better in the newspaper, and it can be mentioned with no shame or dodging the question, at street corners and in shopping malls or in the line at the bank.

When lightning finally strikes angina sufferers on some tragic stormy night, they delve into their chests and clutch with both hands at the knot of their ties while pain rips their grimacing faces. They give the impression that they're doing too much, puffing themselves up with misplaced pride, but they are sincere and we should believe them: that's when the curtain really falls in the theatre of their lives. I'm sincere too, but I don't have the panache of those with a serious heart condition, and I ought to be content with dying from the pelvis, somewhat trivially, following the example of any other young cancer patient. Yes, I squander myself like some birdbrain and in my mouth are regurgitations of bile, but so it goes when you can no longer look behind or deep inside yourself where soon there'll be nothing but a draft and a little puddle of bile.

I'm not spinning a romantic yarn, that's not my style: it's coming, which is all that matters; it's engraved on the sky in letters of flame at the tail of a comet. Oh, no one has dared to admit it but I've guessed everything. I've always known how to scratch the surface of faces and to grasp the thread of muffled terror that vibrates in a voice, and anyway, I'm not totally retarded: for a while now I've been getting all kinds of inexplicable gifts, nice clothes that won't get worn out, Astérix and Tintin books that I've already read a hundred times, all this luxury stuff that I've never even dreamed of, like a little transistor you can slip under your pillow, or a miniature flashlight that brings things to life in the night; and the mailman buries me under clichéd greeting cards from the drugstore, taken from in between aspirins and condoms, cards that seem to be crying farewell to me underneath the good wishes printed in Ontario, and I think that's a sign of the times. I've even had a visit from some kissing cousins, some by marriage, and some others never seen, visits from long-standing uncles and aunts, visitors I usually only see at Christmas, and all that gravity makes me grind my teeth. They could be visitors straight out of a Jack-in-the-box, with their fly-button eyes and their mouths twisted in fear, but the snow was missing, and the night between the stars, and the heavy snow and the air that cuts our faces, and the little colored lights twisted around the balcony railing and the scent of the fir tree decorated with gold balls and sil-ver garlands and an aluminum angel at the feather-duster top of the tree; and the laughing and the drinking songs were absent too, and the pigs' feet stew and the alcoholic bûche de Noël; but above all, above everything else, there was no crèche with the little legendary figures.

It's unreal to see all these Christmas visitors turn up in the middle of September, the month of dead leaves, wild ducks, and chokecherries. They don't coincide with any known image and they move like smoke in their rainboots or in a bad family movie. Unless I'm the surprise baby Jesus this year. . . . (For that matter, the hiss of a radiator warms me like the breath of an ox; and when I call for the nurse at night, a little red light comes on over my bed, like the star of the Magi.) But who knows: maybe a baby Jesus is born on Earth every day and another dies right away in the night, on the other side of the world, so that nobody's jealous, so that every nation thinks they're the chosen people and keeps churning out bibles. No, we never know anything about anything, but while we wait it's pissing rain outside and that disinfects the world.

Strange, but it's here in the hospital that I've learned how to be bored on rainy days and, frankly, it's easier than I thought: you just have to stand with your elbows on the windowsill and think about everything your life could have been if only you'd had a little luck or a little courage. That's the good thing about melancholy: it's a kind of cheap caviar that's within everybody's means. It's crazy, but all this rain is streaming down the windows like torrents of blood. It's as if the sky has burst open with remorse and wants to wash something away, maybe some insult, and people can sense it. Those who come to visit me tremble to the tips of their fingers and are so disoriented they must certainly be sincere, and it saddens me to see them step into my room not knowing where to place their feet or to seat their uneasiness, as if they've swallowed their umbrellas, to say nothing of the appropriate words they try to find in a hat—but if I were them I wouldn't do any better and I bless them with all the grace of the terminally ill. What I appreciate a lot, on the other hand, is that no one tries to roll me in flour like a smelt. The good thing about hospitals: for hygienic reasons, visitors are requested to leave their cat food in the cloakroom. They look washed-out and translucent and no one treats me like a lunatic: the nurses must slip into visitors' eustachian tubes that I'm allergic to dirty tricks.

No, I'm not crazy, just sick, not too much yet, but sick enough, which guarantees that I'll hang on just long enough to arrive at the conclusion of the end, without missing anything. I'm reassured: I will see myself depart. It would have depressed me to miss myself, to perish suddenly without being aware of myself one last time: not to thank myself or any inane thing like that, but just enough to take myself by the hand one last time, to help myself across the threshold of the endless night. My only fear is that a fine mist will fall on the nape of my neck and that I'll feel chilly; I mustn't forget to wear my sweater to my funeral.

At night my eyes close
like paint stores
and in the terrifying night
full stomachs bleed empty stomachs
and the empty stomachs
fill with bare-assed shadows
that will see daylight
under a sky of burnt bread.

Despite the fact that I can see and foresee everything, I can't cry shame like the fucking crybabies who don't even know how to stand up. You have to shut your mouth and put up with the clobbering, sewing your lips shut if necessary. Life eats its young, yes, and then? In the industrial laboratories on the planet, guys in white smocks mash all kinds of fetuses into mush to use in making shampoos to treat male baldness and perfumes for the non-stop female rutting season. And plenty of pathetic countries use their rifles on their own youth. And a whole slew of embryos full of flaws and handicaps end up in the sewers, tasty snacks for rats. And what people has never bombed the kindergartens of a diabolical neighbouring people—who tomorrow will be their best friend? The worst thing is that we can start all over again the next morning if we like, or if we're given the order to do so. Warlords just have to talk about good guys and bad guys and we foam at the mouth right away.

Yes, life eats its young and so what? Who will dare arise and cry, That's enough? No one, of course, given that as far as children are concerned, we eat them all.

> *Secrets are heavy,*
> *the secrets of a worthless man:*
> *you might say*
> *you might say remorse,*
> *remorse for being born.*

In hospital corridors, people walk on eggs with their big fat feet because they carry death inside them. They act naïve, play the offended virgin, but know instinctively the suffering they can cause; they want to shrink out of decency, long enough for a genuflection at the bedside of some hopeless case. But at the foot of the bed I can't really recognize them: it's as if they are filled with shame, humiliated; I see them under a new light and it's appalling. It's easy to see that you are never the person who's placed in a display window for the gallery—and then you wonder who in hell you might be, really. Maybe you are merely what the moment demands you to be, which would amount to saying that each of us is simply one of the billion varieties of a single face grimacing for eternity. You may be nothing more than a bunch of mismatched gestures and facial expressions adrift on an ocean of pleasantries and platitudes, who knows? No, it can't be, there has to be something besides a sick rat at the bottom of the hole—some music, some color, a presence, warmth, maybe a soul, something like humanity and not just a little motor of blind blooddroning on mechanically.

In any event, in my presence, no matter who they are people wear a guilty look like the one on the day after sinning, when they see that, in their eyes, I'm an innocent victim and they're generous enough to confess that they are healthy, but that's never quite right: though they always demean themselves by force, it's easy to see that they are glowing and that joy is within them. So much the better for them and so much the worse for me: the world is what it is and you have to deal with it. What would be most helpful, on the other hand, would be if they were just as they usually are, funny and nice, vulgar enough when needed, serious when appropriate but not for too long, lewd and surprising—perfect, if you will, as usual, and if, above all, they aren't embarrassed to tell me that everything is wonderful with them, that they're swimming in happiness. It would be good for me to hear that, but I'm dreaming in Technicolor because now there is something new in the way we look at one another, something new that confuses everything, that makes things change place within us, pushing some down deeply, bringing others to the surface, and that commotion is a serious source of pain and misunderstanding. And when I half-open my mouth to produce a sound, my visitors drink in my words; thirsty, they need to dip their little buckets to the bottom of my well so they can bring up a little of my spring water, and that intimidates me. Fascinated, I watch as they listen to me, but it doesn't keep me from mulling over a nasty obsession: "Above all, I mustn't say anything stupid . . ."

It's very nice of them to be all ears, they aren't obliged to, but they have their reasons: at the point I've reached any new word is liable to be the last, the one that parents and friends will remember all their lives. For my part, I have to take great care if I want my demise to be equal to their expectations and not let anyone down. You see, I have mountains of pity for them, my nearest and dearest, and in anticipation of their long winter nights I want to leave them some good fatty, plump words with plenty of juicy meat around the marrowbone. So I juggle with all sorts of spiritual last words because I'm well aware that human nature has a short memory and that people mainly remember the end of the show:

shadows bumping into each other behind the curtain, slamming doors, lights going out, and the exit of the dead.

But the trickiest thing for a dying person is to anticipate the precise moment when the current will be switched off. And so if I start to be moved by the flowers in the carpet or mesmerized by the flies on the ceiling, I'm liable not to see the crowbar coming behind my back and I'll exhale a platitude at the crucial moment, meaning that I would have wrecked the dramatic effect of my last words. I know it makes no sense to sacrifice my final days on account of a few miserable words, that's like putting the hearse before the horses or trying to churn the ocean, but I've never had any sense and I certainly won't have any starting today.

No one will be able to save me, better get used to that idea, but make no mistake: deep down, I would have liked to be sad like a normal boy, cross my heart, but I can't do it; it's as if there's a rock at the back of my throat which is blocking the flow, or that I'm a paddle-wheel that's reversing the course of a river.

> *Your Moses-basket carries you*
> *along the river of the world,*
> *towards the lands*
> *of those buried alive,*

and you wonder:
Is after death the same as before life,
dark, empty and silent?
Or is it like the heart
of a tree struck by lightning?

Because of me, lives are turned upside down and it bothers me a lot to upset everyone's routine. My mother has
given up her job, now she can come and see me waste away
a little more every day, with her poor smiles. She tries to be
cheerful, light-hearted, and I see her teeth stained brown by
cigarettes and coffee, but I'm well aware that her heart isn't
in it. I can see that at home, her eyes weep: they're the
unimaginable color of sleepless nights, ringed with the salt
of tears and clouded by small red blood vessels burst into
angels' hair. My mother doesn't want to lose me and I don't
want to lose life, but we lose everything. Though I struggle
against the current in the raging river of the world, I am
myself a world turned upside-down, the scent that returns
to a flower after it has floated around houses, a tree that goes
back into the earth, the stifled cry of men. The universe
wants it, the universe wants me, and I ask myself: can I
really fight with my bare hands those colossal mountains that
scrape against the moon? Sometimes, in front of all the

long, sad faces that come to spoon-feed me their regrets, I feel that I ought to cry, that I'm performing in a melodrama, but I can't help it and everything happens as if nothing will be amiss. It's too close, my snout is pressed against the door of the dead and I still can't see that it's all over.

That's where I am, huddled up in my last entrenched position, because this filthy disgusting thing is ravaging my body: an evil guinea pig is racing like some demented idiot in its rotating cage, in the heart of my guts, and the little Satan is chewing away at my bones, especially my right hip, the wing of my pelvis that has thinned down dramatically with the years. Quite recently a surgeon disembowelled me so as to slip inside my person and scrape my bones with the devil knows what kind of plane. When I woke up in the recovery room where everything is bathed in fluorescent light and moaning, the man seemed quite sorry to tell me that my hip-bone is a sheet of paper; if you stood a candle behind it you would see the flame through the bone and it would have a bleak and terrible beauty. To thank the surgeon for coming to see my disaster in person, I vomited into a chrome basin shaped like a kidney or a suburban swimming pool.

My own poor little hip, my beautiful skate-wing-shaped bone that I loved, that helped me to live my life, that kept me upright during events, is now nothing more than a frail rice-paper Japanese fan. I feel pain all the way to the head of the femur and my sacral vertebrae, but I can't do anything about it and neither can medicine; which means my imminent collapse and decay.

Since that sad medical discovery which will be irrevocably my undoing, I've moved to the hospital where I do my best to make a little home for myself that's welcoming despite the wheelchair parked along the wall, waiting for me like a limousine, ready to take me to new, short-lived adventures. It will never be the most charming bachelor pad though, that's understood, and I sleep in a cold metal bed that seems to be stuffed with prune pits, a weird and hideous bed in which, come night, sleep won't always come because of the sickening smell of drugs where in any case dreams are always monstrous, given the spirit of the place.

Yes, come night the chorus of nightmares covers the entire floor and I sometimes bite my pillow, seeing as how it's often at night that my bones torment me most. In desperation, wincing, I mutter some Hail Mary's along with the Italians who say the evening rosary in the little transistor tucked under my pillow. Other times, when things aren't going too badly, I catch in mid-flight a distant hockey match full of static or listen to music, phone-in shows or the news; I have a weakness for commercials for cars, cheap clothing stores and disgusting restaurants, they make me smile and almost give life a good taste, when I forget myself a little in the night.

Basically, I pretty much don't give a shit about dying, because at the age I am now—nearly seventeen—things aren't moving forward as well as they used to: I look and feel seriously older and I'm afraid that I've already lived the best part of myself, that I've started rambling on and on about the same old things. That's something I really wouldn't have liked—to live my life while bawling over my vanished youth, especially because when you think of it, youth is definitely, not everything, it is a thing and its opposite, a legend and a tall tale; it's nothing but a popular belief, and it's as stupid as folklore.

> *Youth,*
> *is ten when you're twenty;*
> *twenty when you're forty;*
> *forty when you're seventy.*
> *Youth,*
> *is the eternity of halfwits.*

It's funny, but I listen to myself gargling my brains and I understand why my poor psychotherapist worries about my mental health, but I'm unaware, or maybe too aware, I don't know which, but out of this mush I've nonetheless grasped one truth: I will die, yes, but with no hope, no vulgar need to be loved and missed. Maybe, deep down, that's what it means to be a man, a real man, and maybe I've become one without knowing, the way we take sick one night in our sleep, who knows? So it's true: my woes must have started at one specific point, this crappy business isn't something that turns up out of the blue, there must be a zero moment, a bugle call at the first mutation. Maybe I was partway through a hockey game last winter; or maybe I was at school, sweating over a math exam; or maybe it happened in the middle of summer while I was watching my mother cut up a melon; or while I was swimming in the river with my sister and brother; or running through the woods with my dog. In any event, I didn't feel a thing when the Antichrist entered me, when the dark power began to reign over my kingdom. It's a spell that arrived in one breath, a sentence that does not forgive, and it lives on borrowed blood like an enigma, but at least that devastation will have made me into a serious man. The proof is that if I had to choose, I would prefer to be loved by a single woman who is free than by a harem of wives in chains. Isn't that an excellent example of maturity? Insipid and degenerate like no one else, I'm prepared to go on television, but that's just a manner of speaking: basically, I've lost the urge to be seen as I am and I would like to pass away in secret, in my dark corner; just die like a dog, but I'll have to be satisfied to die like a man, which is in any case a fine effort.

By the way, my psychotherapist's name is Maryse, Maryse Bouthillier, and she told me that her family name is very old, a thousand years old, that it comes from the Grand Échanson de la Bouteillerie of King Philip I. (An *échanson* is someone who serves beverages, according to Maryse's *Petit Larousse* dictionary, between *échangiste* or swinger and *échantillon* or sample.)

Maryse Bouthillier is a real hospital shrink, who dresses impeccably and is very serious. From a distance she seems a little cold, but close-up she's a sweetheart, with her gemstone eyes and her translucent nose in the shape of a Lima bean. She smells of I don't know what, some kind of spice or bark or a flower from Africa, and it smells good when she leans across my life to roll up the pillow against the wall and help me rest against it in my bed. After that, we exchange remarks, but I don't take it in all that well because my mind is elsewhere. I blush a little at whispering the reason but here it is: secretly I can see a bit of Maryse's breasts in the opening of her blouses and it's a true commencement of a universe that is being offered to me, nearly a biblical beginning that could turn me into a believer, but I don't say anything. That's because I'm not yet altogether legally a man before the courts, but still a teenager who doesn't want to end up stuck between two skins; and the age and social distance from Maryse Bouthillier keep me from opening my mouth, but I accept her silent female offering like money at mass, which is money that's handed out for free.

"Mama, how much does money cost?"

"A lot. It costs an arm and a leg."

That's a childhood memory which explains why for a long time I thought that anyone missing a limb was rich, which I tell my shrink who's very fond of anecdotes and autobiographies, O Maryse of my sighs who must see me looking down her perfumed neckline, I can't believe that she doesn't. We may be sick but we don't die every day, and when I'm feeling good I must have a comical squint, like the Missisquoi Bay sunfish of my childhood. Anyway, a woman must have a tingling sensation on her bosom when a man does something like love her from afar, with prominent shining eyes; and the cloud that brushes against her must tickle her skin, but the woman who cares for my invisible bleeding is a shrink, and my puberty mustn't be the kind of mutation that she finds too alarming, she's probably been through quite a lot or I wouldn't be one of her cases. But maybe she thinks that I'm checking out the little badge with her name engraved on it, or her unusual necklace that attracts the light, or else she thinks that I am drifting in a dream of God, head full of the nothingness of the higher realms, given the no-win situation in which my barefoot destiny will lose its way, in the smoke of the galaxies. The worst thing is that she's hardly ever wrong: it's true that I sometimes think deep thoughts about the Eternal, but never for long because the burning hurts too much. Yes, God, that's what happens; I learned it with the pain that's eating away at me. Still, breasts are beautiful female mysteries from the lands of milk and honey, and I'd have happily lived a life of spiritual and physical communion, but there you are, I'll never experience the infinite Sunday of a happy life with a naked woman who loves me and whom I love in my bed. It's because I'm still a tiny bit too young and it's a tiny bit too late on the great clock of things. It makes me so mad I could spit: I came within inches of aging until I became the man so devoutly hoped-for, and arrived at the feet of the promised woman, but *that* great secret I'll take with me into the earth—another one, and it breaks my heart. I wouldn't have harmed any women; I would have asked them how to love them in detail and I'd have behaved according to what they said. Yes, I weep to see these hands of mine, so well made to fit the shape of breasts and women's bodies, but I will die poor, empty-handed, with my heart stewed like a rabbit, and I will be lifeless in the dust without the dead beauty lying at my side.

It's hard to believe, but if I'd been Maryse Bouthillier's age I might one day have kissed her between the nose and chin, right where it would create a little electric shock on the edge of her unwilling lips, but I'll never be any age except the age I am today, and just thinking about it sends a chill down my spine; I've already come to the end of my rope, like a baby goat that has already nibbled its ring of dandelions. But I think that Maryse Bouthillier really is fond of me, professionally fond I mean, and I'm more than fond of her, mine is a sick fondness that's drawing to an end, but it's better than nothing, and I always wait for her eagerly, horizontally in my bachelor pad. She often drops in, you see, so I can cheer her up and it makes me happy to encourage her. Anyway, at the point I've reached, it's free. I can't afford now to be demanding or to ask for any-thing but a scrap of pity, and I'd really like to take advantage of my dying days to the very last drop of IV solution: I've paid a high price, it cost me a fortune and the work of a lifetime, and I want a fair return for all the money earned by the cold sweat of my brow. I am entirely within my victim's rights and the Nazi euthanasist who'd refuse me that hasn't been born yet.

Besides her ruddy complexion and her coffee-colored eyes, she has two beautiful children clinging to her comethair, that's Maryse my shrink I'm talking about, children she's given birth to in a photo where a man she once had but doesn't any more is smiling, she must have lost him in her paperwork somewhere, or between two appointments, either that or she was lost by him because he loved somewhere else, which can happen in the best of families, but what Maryse Bouthillier sees on my face will help her to love those children even more, to love them forever and deeply, and that's what I want for her as a dear and faithful friend. After all, my deep undying love isn't an empty promise, and at least I'll have been able to inspire something greater than myself in someone older than me; it will be the bravery medal pinned onto my gooseflesh. Not bad for a guy made infertile by his nitrogenic mustards, the cyclophosphamides that I savor in the form of 50 milligram pills. Circumstances will have made me sterile, but I've always had a weakness for sterility, it's as if from birth, my days were drowned in the mists of time, and ever since, I've been drinking the sour milk of solitude, an incurable solitude that I hide from everyone, even my best friends, but that I take with me everywhere, like the shadow of a cross.

On the other hand, I'm nosier than a weasel and I'll

always wonder what it's like to have children who stare at you like the destitute and can't live without you, who have to be fed and cuddled, kept safe from smallpox and myelitis so you can bring them up to the height of a man, and who cry for real when you depart. Still, it's rare that a human being can't live without someone else, even for lovers it's uncommon, the proof floats all around in the light, save perhaps among old folks who don't have anything or anyone and don't even have a horizon anymore; but I guess that's the magic of childhood.

I will always wonder too what it would be like to be happy, I who am unable to believe in happiness: for me, happiness is a bunch of stories that we tell ourselves to put ourselves to sleep, and if it's useful for that it's still only words, and words don't know what there really is deep inside our solitude. No, it's not happiness that leads to the heart of man, it's something else, I don't know what, it's the man himself, or better: the woman.

It's a strange thing to see, a separated shrink walking graciously down the hallway with an accordion file under her arm. Maryse Bouthillier has her own style and way of speaking; she walks with the sway of a domesticated vamp; she has a lovely personality that is carefully tended to the fingertips, and I can always recognize her footsteps in the distance because of her wooden heels that ring out like the bars of a xylophone, and I like the music of her silver bracelets. She has kohl on her eyelashes, cheeks like fruit, a neck filled with shivers of light; her naked arm bears the beautiful lunar crater of a vaccination, but also a bruise on her finger—the one wearing the permanently ephemeral wedding ring that wounded her flesh, and I thought to myself, she has lived so she must know what she's talking about. I also tell myself that she is a free woman and my heart bleeds because I'm not her beloved.

Sometimes when my shrink, with her expensive perfume, her silvery voice and her fawn's breath, sits beside me to talk about life, I watch her raspberry lips move and I'm within a hair's breadth of asking permission to lightly touch her unimaginable breast, but I behave myself, I sit there calmly and answer her complicated questions any old way, and when it comes time for me to reveal my secrets so that it's a real therapy, what I do is, I lie, but I mean well, cross my heart, and it's the best thing I can do to reassure her. Yes, I lie, but it's another way of loving her way of thinking, and seemingly perfectly innocent, I admire her throat that's the color of the heart of a strawberry; and anyway it does a man good, lying, it brings him a little closer to the true nature of a woman who's so difficult to touch, I want to talk about woman's dizzying heights, where the air is thinner, where man has to search for his breath. And I confess that it makes hordes of butterflies hatch in my stomach, lying to a woman, especially to a smart psychotherapist. You tell yourself that she must know that we know that she knows, which forges sentimental ties. It's very delicate, a wire above some flames, but what I like most about her is that she isn't the least bit straight-laced: she sees me at the level of dust bunnies with others of my kind.

Before, when I was going to school, I was as transparent as the heavens and the girls didn't see me; their ultraviolet gazes ran right through me and I felt like the surface of a stream; but now that I'm passing slowly away from the bones I've become a young man who is seen, looked at in spite of his nondescript appearance, even examined from every angle on certain days, and frankly, I'm not picky, I take whatever is going around: it gives me the illusion that I'm somebody, which soothes the wounded heart for as long as it lasts, even if it's never pleasant to be forced to feel sorry for having been spotted in the gap of an existence, deep down in the sordid reality of this world.

The other day, I racked my brains until I finally understood what my marvelous psychotherapist really wants from me, beneath her smooth face and behind her crystal pupils:

she hopes to help me shed some light on my darkness, to name the painful feelings, the powerful and never named emotions, that wheel perhaps like vultures in my tragic sky, in spirals of distant planets that may horrify the sensitive man and cause him to die on the wrong foot.

It's true that it's not a bad idea to tidy one's portrait, to put some polish on the soul and on the shoe before stepping into eternity, but there's no way that I'll deteriorate to the whimpering of the cosmic uterus, I have my dignity; so I was wondering if her fine proposal has anything to do with me now. If it's not for me, I said, for whom would I do it? Ms. Thing wouldn't answer me and that pinched my pride. I fired a little dazzling black lightning from my eyes and seethed for a tremorous moment, exasperated but unaware that I was the plaything of a craftiness that has worked very well: I finally broke the ice and spoke the truth for once, to open a new era between us. Yes, I threw myself into chitchat and rather surprised my favorite shrink by declaring that the absolute end isn't as totally dark as you might think. For instance, I explained to her that oblivion can be learned, which is a good thing for others; that it teaches me that I'm not God's gift to mankind, to erase myself mathematically from the universe, in a sparseness without religion where you can finally catch your breath, and frankly, I find that it's a tremendous relief from the unending tension of the ego trained on my own image from the cradle, since my very first day in this world of fools.

She scribbled some notes on hospital paper with a university pen, frowning and clinking her silver bracelets. I enjoyed seeing her quickly darken pages with her spidery scrawl: I thought that I'd be playing a role in her Ph.D. thesis, very soon, and that thanks to me, my psychotherapist would earn a higher salary some day.

Ah yes, lepers flatter themselves as best they can.

After that I had some other true facts for her in my bag of mischief, where awaited me the man who made me what I am, who did what he could with what he had; and when I was ready to betray myself, I began by saying that my father's visits encouraged me a lot, because basically I think I'm lucky: I am dying just in time and I won't have to live the life he's lived, he won't pass on the human weaknesses that the near future had in store for me. That's because my poor father has always shot like an arrow into the darkness of his existence, without admiring the landscape or smelling the flowers, and he doesn't know that there are meadows for picnics in the summer, frozen ponds for skating in the winter, maple syrup springs and the preserves of autumn. I wouldn't want to have his skin on my bones, the skin of a bookkeeper which is his idiotic profession. He spends his whole life except Sunday in the cellar of a furniture warehouse, where he does nothing that his heart asks him to do. I hate to think about the human sorrow that practically tears me apart, more than any physical pain, but I know that my father's dreams will end in the thunderclap of a heart attack. His heart is a time bomb, given his family history, given the heart of my grandfather Langlois stuffed with nitroglycerin; he died before I was born, heart exploding like a grenade, so that if I stick my ear to the floor to find out what's coming I can already hear the earth quaking.

My father's most loathsome flaw is loyalty: he has always done what others have wanted him to do, but what's most heartbreaking is that he does it better than anyone, otherwise he wouldn't be sitting on the same chair in the same cellar for twenty years, among the cockroaches, in the lighted circle of a small hanging lamp like a Chinese peasant's hat. It's as if my father were waiting for a miracle in the half-light, for the arrival on earth of an archangel of freedom, but he does nothing to help himself: his morale is often in his feet and he's afraid of being a man who once believed. The thing is, he tragically lacks faith in the man he could become if he really wanted to, which is something that affects me very deeply. If the eyes are the mirror of the soul, my father's

eyes are a two-way mirror, because I've never seen a shadow
of a soul reflected in them. It's not that he doesn't have one,
but it's padlocked deep inside the individual where it dies,
and only tremors rise into the hands of that man. My poor
father, so kind, so tired, so helpless. He deserves better than
that. I feel like telling him, "Papa, stop searching, stop waiting: I am your miracle, your angel of liberty . . ."

I hope that my modest death will shake up my father and
tip him over to the side where people have some kind of life.
It's the least a man can hope for from the death of one of his
children.

Here, we are a batch of chicks all nestled under the warm
wing of the hospital, mother of us all. At night sometimes
when I think about various things with my eyes wide open,
I can detect a persistent throbbing sound that makes everything quiver, like an emotion that spreads into the walls, and
it's the hospital that lives all around us, which is reassuring;
I feel like one of those kittens that snuggle up against an
alarm clock, thinking the tick-tock is the heartbeat of the
mother they've lost.

At night, through the windows of my bachelor pad, I can
see the thick smoke that escapes, seething, from a very tall

brick chimney behind an old hospital building, and I wonder if it's there, safe from the eyes of disheartened patients, that attendants burn the gangrenous legs, the bunches of fistulous lymph nodes, the long sections of colons, and all the organs assaulted by tumors, all the blackened flesh ripped out of the carcasses of patients riddled with the cancers that roam the world and swoop down on innocent prey, devouring their lungs, intestines, prostates, uterus, breasts, liver, brain. The healthy man can't imagine all the potential pain he has inside him, which is just as well, because it allows him to exist without banging his head against the walls, but I possess the fire of knowledge, which I've stolen from the gods, and I tremble at the thought that soon it may be my turn to go up in flames in pieces, in those crematorium furnaces beneath the brick chimney, and that I'll go up in smoke into the firmament above the city where I've lived, through the lanes where I've played ball and hockey, where I learned to ride a bike with no knowledge of the facts; but I try for some consolation by reminding myself that my friends, my parents, my brother, and my sister will perhaps inhale me in the early hours, that they will breathe in my smoke on their way to work or school, taking me far away with them into their lives, their flesh, dissolved in their warm blood.

At the point I've reached—I mean, already a little behind things, a little above the crowd—a person thinks about all kinds of useless things, stirring our brains hard enough to give us meningitis, but sometimes we find something lying on the ground or drifting in the air, a supposition or a theory, say, and we pick it up as if it were a fledgling that's fallen from the nest, which is how one night I picked up a belief: the notion that body and spirit form two beings who've hated each other from time immemorial, but are forcibly reunited by I don't know what kind of black magic, by a sort of malevolent gravity, an infernal earthly attraction. Over time, one of those two unhappy beings has become the slave of the other, I mean the soul is the slave of the body, and that's why the soul can no longer become manifest in the visible world, and why it allows itself to be humiliated by the body, which devotes itself to all the unimaginable filth and obscenities, and that's why no one ever shows himself to others in all his purity; instead, each of us indulges in soiling, in calculating, in betraying because of the body, which tortures the spirit and spits on it. And which also explains why the down-and-out soul suffers in the realm of the sick.

I'm in such bad shape that it's with such thoughts of madness that I stun myself when I writhe like a lettuce worm in my sagging bed; more often though, I stupidly ask myself what use

I've been, what use I will be, as if I belonged in the can-opener, cheesecloth, or kitchen tongs family. The worst thing is that I come up with answers. O Greater Omentum . . . where do we come from? . . . O Gog, king of Magog . . . where are we going? . . . We come from there and we're going there . . . or maybe the reverse. Everything is possible or impossible.

"O TV shows of my childhood, O Fanfreluche, O Boîte à surprises, who am I?"

Say, that's the first time I've spoken in ages and it feels very weird to hear my voice resonating inside me as if I were in a stairwell. It's enough to make me wonder if I'm still inhab-ited, if there is still a living soul within my depths.

"O Pollux and Zebulon, O Thor and Pharaoh, come and see if I'm there."

I may clown around, but I know everything: I'm still alive and playing the part of the one in a million against whom others measure their luck and realize that they're com-plaining over apple seeds. No one talks about it, no one says so, but I wouldn't be surprised to find out that plenty of men make better love to their wives after they've seen my face in the hospital (maybe not the same night, given their modesty, or the next day, given their remorse, but let's say two days later), I who know so well how to bring out the best in life through contrast. Yes, I'm convinced that I secretly help a bunch of husbands who are usually a little abrupt in bed, all tangled up as they are in their matrimonial life and their ordinary lies, but who, if forced to see the reality of things because of my collapse, start to think that their own lives aren't so bad after all and discover tenderness and sweet surrender in the arms of a wife whom, in fact, they love more than they'd realized. With that, you may applaud me. I accept donations, but the fact remains that it's true: if the only useful thing I've done is that—I mean to encourage lovemaking by couples who were starting to seriously get on one another's nerves and whose brains were tickled by the thought of divorce or adultery—well, I would fly off happily at my Assumption, with a lovely smile like the one on a little plaster saint stuck to my lips.

Speaking of love, one night I listened to a little bit of opera on my transistor's FM just to see, and I liked it; I liked it so much that the next day I sang in a terrible way, that's right, I sang about love, *l'amour, toujours l'amourrr*. Love, love is a rebel bird, that never, ever has known a law! . . . My voice is rich: it disgusts people quickly. People bombarded me with slippers and pillows to shut me up, but I had time to think again about the little school where my first love rang the bell, a real hand bell that shone in the sunlight in the schoolyard.

Ah! what has become of you, O my first life? . . . I close my eyes and I hear tinkling in the distance, but what's that false note from the bell? It's broken: there's no schoolmistress at the end of it now. The bells are asleep in bell towers . . . schoolmistresses in bellflowers . . . a lover under their skirts, like a horsefly that bites or an idea that gains ground, but a chalkless schoolmistress doesn't fly very high, like a ladybug without wings, but without wings am I still in love with her? . . . The sad response is back there in an inkwell at the end of childhood, with the message that I've never dared to write her. It dried up in my queasy heart and it was: will you marry me? Ah! I, who wanted to be everything for her, am nothing even for my dog! I am dying in secret, like a sparrow, and in the dust where I have fallen, children sneeze all the way to hooky school where they count on their fingers and on their toes in order to get to twenty. One, two, three, I'm dangling from a tree . . . four, five, six, next to Christ, that's quite a fix . . . seven, eight, nine, who is no friend of mine . . . ten, eleven twelve . . . What! I've got twelve fingers! I'm a bandit! I've stolen two from someone who has eight! That doesn't count! Me too, I want to be resurrected! Mademoiselle Villemure, answer me, will you marry me? It's me who's asking you, yes, me, the impenitent thief poisoned by sin, for I am the biblical evil. Deliver me from the Book! It's

so cold in the shadow of the church . . . but I'll steal communion wine to christen our hot-air balloon . . . Oh, Mademoiselle, let's fly away into the sun where you'll be even more
my teacher, let's run away to the stars where you will rescue
me. Mademoiselle Villemure . . . Do you know what place
you occupy in the whirlwind of my childhood school mornings? But you also taught me about suffering and jealousy,
one autumn day when I spotted you in the supermarket on
the arm of a man brought back from summer vacation. You
were buying apples and you were happy, do you remember?
Ah, love . . . love isn't a bird, it's a son of a bitch!

I often need an injection, especially before a biopsy, and
the drugs are ones that cause euphoria, like love—but when
I'm myself again I often vomit.

"And who's going to see my ass?"

"Nobody, just me."

"Do you swear on the godhead?"

"I swear."

That had better be true, Auntie, otherwise watch out, I'll
boycott your needles and your blood tests, and the hospital
will go broke. No way will I let just anybody see my two
cheatskin moons.

The nurses, we call them all "auntie" to create an illusion,
to create a little family connection that can't do any harm.

"Your grandfather just arrived, son . . . He's on his way . . . Here he is . . ."

Grandpa! Oh, Grandpa Baillargeon, it really is you. That's it, already I'm a different man. First of all, footsteps like heart-beats, breathlessness that is the shock of joy, then a shadow in the doorway where my existence hangs by a thread, a dark-ness in the shape of a man I love, with a nervous hat in his hand. Rowboats with soles and heels, a scarf that loves the wind, overcoat and trousers shiny from wear, shaving-brush bristles in the nostrils, ears that look good enough to chew, huge dark bottle-thick glasses. Big hands, hairy and full of feelings that hover around the hat. A hesitation that sniffs and blows its nose but above all, above everything else, a chest like a buffalo's full of affection for his grandson who won't be around long enough to let him down or scandalize him. Let's swallow our anger and praise the Lord, it's now or never.

My grandfather's pockets are always full of little clove-flavored goldfish, blessed be he.

Grandpa, I'm beside myself with joy when I'm not expecting anyone and all at once you tumble from the sky like a prophet falling off a shooting star; it's a wonderful surprise when you burst onto the scene in your headgear ornamented with the feather of a warbler.

It's funny, though I'm fairly close to turning seventeen

and I've got all my wisdom teeth, I still get a lump in my throat when my grandfather kisses me on the forehead and holds me against his shoulder. It makes me melt and it practically cures me, yes, practically, which in the state that I'm in means a lot.

"How's Grandma?"

"Not so bad . . . She'll be coming on Sunday . . ."

Sunday, always Sunday, only Sunday. It's the one day that grandparents have in their mouths and it makes me sad for them: they're bored with their lives and wish that we'd visit them more often, but there you are, weekends are for karate, swimming, hockey, piano; we're very busy enlightening the leisure society, which means that in a few years we'll park the grandparents in an old folks' home so we can have some blessed peace, because keeping in your house old folks who ramble and soil themselves is no leisure activity. Luckily I won't be around to see that deportation.

I remember one day hearing my grandfather Baillargeon declare that there aren't thirty-six kinds of misery, there are only two: youth and old age. We live or we die, that's all, and those are the only real kinds of misery in the world, was what he said. Anyway, to him poets are fearful people who live with their brains in the sky, along with some weird birds that flutter around the sun, which is the center of their universe, and they never do anything good in life, unlike manual laborers who know what to do in any circumstance without being pleased with themselves, who don't fear real life which is dingy, dirty, and inglorious, and so full of genuine suffering to be relieved all around them, no farther away than the corner of the street or the next room. What is most dignified about all humankind, and what is the only noble thing to do here on earth according to my grandfather, is to live as if nothing were wrong, as if we saw nothing looming on the horizon; and those who are well have to take care of those who are unwell while they wait to be unwell themselves and that's that. Nothing there to foul up any poems. Of course my grandfather no longer talks about such things since I myself have become all the miseries on earth, since I've been poeticizing my poor elementary reality, and I know he'd be ashamed if he knew that I remember one particular Sunday, ashamed at having talked through his hat too much even though I think he's right and, to prove it to him, I don't say anything serious, I talk about the weather in the name of the love that binds us, as if I couldn't see anything looming, and I hope he realizes it.

"Is it nice out?"

"Chill . . . There's a bit of wind . . ."

Yes, outside a bit of fatal wind is blowing on your country which I can see through the window and a strange country it is, Grandpa, where the affluent whimper like sissies, where two and two don't make four as they do elsewhere, where the devastated countryside is a shambles of vinyl and aluminum, where clear-cut villages resemble piles of shoe boxes that are baking in the sun or suffocating under the snow, where cities are warts, where schools look like factories, where everything could happen but nothing ever does; and if I weren't going to die a natural death I wonder if at the age of twenty I would have considered blowing my brains out like all the young people in this sad grey country, Grandpa. At the same time, though, it's a country that is looking after me, that can't do very much but still wants to relieve my pain, and will hope for a miracle until the end; it's a country that feeds me, washes me, smiles at me, and would like to see me go back to school; a country that tries out insane surgical procedures but will pay the astronomical bill without balking; a naïve country that wants so much to do good that it manages to move me; a country that I love in spite of everything because it's the one where I opened my eyes and where I will close them. In my lifetime I'll have seen only the light of Canada, the stars of Missisquoi Bay, and the moon in the parking lots of malls swept by winter winds; and I'll have been caressed by the sun that people carry around inside themselves like a blessed sacrament.

Oh Grandpa, I may look as if I'm trying to be independent off here by myself, but if you only knew how bad things are you'd understand everything. Grandpa, do you think it's possible that I might wake up one fine morning with my disease all washed away to the whiteness of my bones, purified to the soul, brand new and fresh as a daisy?

Sometimes, Grandpa, I have glimmers of hope that blind me and I think I've been cured, but what can I say, put yourself in my place: it's not my fault if man is some poor guy who thinks that his leprosy is lace.

No, it's not my fault if I'm a man. To tell the truth, it could even be a bit of your truth, Grandpa, but I forgive you, with a magical gesture I erase all your sins except the ones that you're really attached to.

I recognize my shadow in the shadow of my grandfather, my own trembling in his hands, my ignorance in his eyes. I have no doubts about the origin of species.

■

I haven't said anything yet about the most hideous days, the days when the pain rips me open and leave my eyes scalding and glassy, my face decomposed, my bones bare and my forehead greasy and my dirty hair clings to it like seaweed and my damp pajamas stink of sweat. When the nurses come to turn my bed upside down so they can bleach the sheets in which I've sweated blood and lymph, I'm always afraid they'll discover a Turin Shroud that would dehumanize me, like some kind of Easter Sunday, like the resurrection of Christ who spoiled everything by erasing the pain of the Passion, by canceling the sacrifice of Good Friday.

No one comprehends the fact that there are times when I feel like killing everybody, that I often need to spit on anything that moves, to be more cruel than ever, I mean when I feel that I'm finished, like a rat, that the lion's mouth is closing on a fatal night, and that I can no longer bear the lives of others, those carefree people all puffed up with life expectancy which is the measure of what is possible—but it's nothing, nothing, just the bitterness of a dying man that is rising up from deep in my guts along with my bad faith. Take it easy, take it easy, repeats like a parrot the bald *abbé* who limps down the corridors on his goat-headed cane, not knowing that it's the devil himself he is warming up with his hand, the hypocritical Abbé Guillemette who's always telling me that I've got a good head on my shoulders so that later on, he can lead me astray with his nebulous teachings— don't worry, life is more wonderful, death is less harsh than you think, blablabla. But it's a downright stupid obsession: because I refuse to believe in their artificial and enticing world, they all insinuate that I'm wrong, that I'm seeing things, which is wrong on two counts, given that we all sink into error like anvils and as for seeing things, I already did that when I was seven so now I'm immune.

Here in the hospital, I'm encircled by a whole crown of sick friends whose destiny resembles mine, but to a certain point only, which is a fork in the road where each of us turns onto his last lonely stations of the cross, which is why, at the end, we don't all die in the same way: some will have a hard time of it, like dying dogs, all the way to the edge of the grave, while others will scarcely feel the caress of the mainsail on their cheeks. The best thing is that a few, miraculously cured, will pull through by the skin of their teeth, with all the honors, for instance my friend Louis in the next room.

Last week, the surgeons dissected him and then they sewed up the tear that this delightful boy had, a genuine hole in his heart, like a saint's made by a lance smack in the old ticker. That was because, before his operation, floods of dirty blood from his right ventricle were defiling the good clean blood in the left ventricle, which came from his lungs, and the defective pump was sending the poisoned blood into his aorta. He was suffering from some kind of blue sickness that in the long term, slowly but surely, is fatal, but now that Louis's been fixed, he works better than a new man, and his well-oiled heart purrs inside his chest like a little dynamo that sends out sparks all the way to his eyes, like the heart of a saint. The secret is that they've put up a little wall in his mended heart and created zones inside it: an imperial city for the pure blood, a brothel for the hybrid. No mixing, because the heart is a monarchy; it is the seat of our emotions.

"It's probably psychological," Louis told me, "but it's as if something's tickling me in the heart."

"It is? . . . Maybe you should talk to Maryse Bouthillier, she's pretty good with mental things."

"Okay, I'll see, but meanwhile the blood is creating vibrations in the violin string they sewed me up with and the worst thing is, I can't even scratch myself."

"Who says that it isn't butchers' string?"

"No, it's a violin string, the highest pitched, the E-string."

He's always surprising me, Louis the clown, who also says that they crushed his ribcage like a lobster claw and that after the open-heart surgery, they closed him up with chicken wire.

"When I rotate my shoulders, I can feel it playing in the crunchy part."

He means that the cartilage in his sternum cracks and that the wire tries to pierce the skin, but he says you get used to it.

"Better a ticker that gets on your nerves than one that doesn't tick at all," I replied.

Oh, it's fine to fiddle with words, but it's a struggle, and the hundred dollar question is always hanging in the air: how do you scratch an itchy heart? The answer is hidden in a divinatory biscuit like a maxim of Confucius, the favorite philosopher of Chinese restaurants.

> *An itchy heart*
> *is a caged love*
> *that beats the seconds*
> *of another's scalding blood.*

In a week's time, my little saint Louis will leave the hospital with his heart set free and vibrating with music that he'll use for loving an unhoped-for girl, but while he's waiting for the love that hops up to the corner of the street. My friend will spend his free time celebrating our memory, recounting our tragic epic to friends who won't believe their ears: the appalling story of some poor lost souls who haven't had much luck and who will have croaked before the normal time, before death no longer scandalizes anyone, I mean the death of old folks that makes people yawn; and we, the chosen of the sacrifice to the moon, we'll cage ourselves forever in the heads of over-sensitive children. But that may not be doing them a favor and I wonder, finally, if the survivors wouldn't be better off silencing the hard times that will have fallen on us.

A small miracle the other morning: I wasn't expecting anything when my destiny crossed the destiny of a girl I felt right away I'd get along with. A little embarrassed at being a boy and a girl who seem to have an urge to talk but are pretending that nothing is happening we waited wheel to wheel, in silence, in a special room on our floor where they come to get you and take you somewhere else, often to the guts of the hospitals where all kinds of huge and horrible machines rumble and roar and bombard us with all kinds of penetrating rays that give you something to think about. For me, it was going to be X-rays to photograph my lungs, and for her, gamma rays to burn her spleen, which is as huge as a big bloody cob of corn.

Suddenly our sidelong glances got tangled up like kites and we became friends through force of circumstance. I introduced myself as best I could, mumbling, but she passed over my nervousness to tell me that her name was Marilou, Marilou Desjardins, and then she recounted the tragedy of her life to get it over with as fast as possible and move on to something better between us.

"A few years ago, at my confirmation, my grandparents gave me a beautiful watch with numbers and hands that glowed in the dark, like the souls of those who have been saved, but you mustn't trust it because that light is lethal, like the light from atomic bombs, and the radioactive rays destroyed the blood in my wrist, around the watch, and the disease spread through my whole body and one morning I woke up with leukemia."

It sends shivers up your spine to know that it started with the absence of menstruation, that they then examined her blood all the way down to the corpuscles, and they discovered some abnormal cells with Philadelphia chromosomes. That's what they're called, said Marilou, who was perhaps going to live in spite of everything, but the oncologists didn't yet dare to say so: they're as cautious as the blind and you can understand that they don't want to play with other people's fire. While waiting to read any kind of future in Marilou's entrails, they go to a lot of trouble to exterminate all the white corpuscles that are on the blink and treat her with chemical hope, but without sugar-coating the pill.

"How about you, what've you got?"

"An osteosarcoma and six chances in ten of being toast."

I explained to her that it usually builds its nest in the knee but that I'm a nonconformist.

"My sarcoma wormed its way in between my crotch and my butt."

I waited for a while, but nothing. I'd thought that mentioning my butt would elicit a laugh, but no. She sat there, pensive, Marilou, but I didn't get discouraged.

"There's one thing I've learned here that reassured me a lot: I'm not allergic to the color yellow . . ."

Now that took her out of herself and her problems a little, and I explained.

"In my cyclophosphamide pills there's number five yellow which could have caused an allergic reaction, but I'm okay . . . I won't have to throw out my Phentex slippers . . ."

She checked out my feet and finally she smiled; but best of all was that as one thing led to another, we discovered that we both write poetry, and that united us in the invisible. And then the guy I was waiting for rushed in to abduct me and take me far away, into the catacombs of the third basement, and Marilou and I arranged to meet later, to read the lines in our hands.

My rickety rickshaw pusher seemed to have sparrows in his belly, so loudly did it gurgle in the elevator (where my ears were level with his stomach), but it's nothing, he told me, just flatulence.

Way down in the cellar there awaited the attendant responsible for radiation, whose name is Robert and who's something of a clown. I know him well: we've been seeing each other for weeks in the midst of particles; he's always the one who fires the cobalt guns, the electron accelerators, and other weapons of war at me.

"Hi there, big boy, how's it going?"

I told him it would be going better if I were normal, but that I was trying to make the best of a bad situation, to see if it was possible, but when you can hold your whole fortune in the palm of your hand, you could say that the situation made you feel like jumping off the roof.

"Hang in there, big boy, we'll beat this thing."

To play down his everyday existence as a gatekeeper, Robert cracks jokes the way others crack their knuckles or lick the corners of their lips: he was infected so long ago that he's no longer aware of the pain.

"You'll see," he told me as he settled me in my chair like a puppet in front of the plate. "This is one of those big machines filled with women's gazes that pierce our secrets all the way to the bone. You'll get stared at like you've never been stared at in your blessed life."

I told him I know, I'm used to it. Once, I drank some kind of milk thickened with chalk and an X-ray technician filmed me with his magic lantern while I swallowed it. On the screen I was a moving skeleton, and I felt as if my little bones would sound like a xylophone, and I could see a membrane throbbing, my transparent heart that looked like a jellyfish gently swollen by sighs, and I'd swallowed the contents of their bariumed bottle and I felt like screaming it was so horrible to see myself like that—a little bundle of bones without a soul, more skinned than bare-assed, more flayed than a rotting carcass.

"Okay, stay like that, hold still . . ."

Robert placed me artistically so that the X-ray would be a good likeness, then he ran and hid behind his armored glass partition where I watched him watching me.

"Okay, now give me a nice smile!"

I smiled as a joke when the little birdie popped out, but it didn't really come from the heart, it came from a little lower down and on the right, from my melancholy liver; and the invisible thunderbolt caught by surprise two ghosts inside me, my lungs that worry me, that may have some nasty idea in mind such as the shadow of a doubt. It's too depressing me to think that a tumor weighing one gram contains a billion malignant cells. It makes for a crowd at mass and quite a few mouths to feed; most of all, it makes you wonder if you can hold your own before the Eternal.

For the balance of the day I rested and in the afternoon, I heard on the radio that scientists were going to analyze samples from the Shroud of Turin. I thought it would be like a biopsy of Christ two thousand years after the fact, which would be risky for religion: they may find out that Jesus died of cancer like everybody else. His star could fade and the Book of Books could drop to the bottom of the best-seller list.

At nightfall, dressed in my best striped pajamas and stylishly shod in yellow Phentex slippers knitted by my grandmother Langlois, I traveled by limousine to my date and I observed that yes indeed, Marilou is to my liking, that she's not *as beautiful as the day is long*, but a thousand times more so, and that if the day were a rose, Marilou would be a whole bouquet. She is so beautiful that the poor little day doesn't come up to her ankle. All beauty is blasphemy, they say, I mean you hear that from men who hate life, so we have to blaspheme like the damned, from the depths of the earth to the summit of Heaven, and I blaspheme until I run out of breath, until my eyesight disappears at the feet of Marilou, my dear little Rilou who looks like an Indian with her Mongolian cheekbones, her hazelnut eyes, and her long black hair, so black that it turns midnight blue in the light. I thought about the Attikamekw, the Dogrib, or the

Cheyenne who are tribes that set me dreaming, but it's Abenaki blood that flows in her veins, the blood of someone close to her, rich grandmother blood, which explains her love of a sacred turtle that she keeps in the house, a turtle called Coquecigrue, that she scooped up with a net among the reeds in the Saint-François River, the mythic turtle of the Abenaki that scrapes the horizons of the earth with its flat belly and takes a cast of Heaven with its bulging carapace. We learn something every day and I love that. Alas, Marilou's good Abenaki blood has turned to celery juice in her veins, which is not a guarantee of longevity, anyway she often has an upset stomach so I didn't bother her for long that night. But she made me promise to come back and see her some other afternoon.

I left with a kind of cake of leafy poems on my knees and I read them that night, which made me feel better. They opened my eyelids onto her universe, one that includes mine, because even though Marilou is just fifteen, she's already writing things that blow me away, that are way better than mine, like the poem that talks about rest for the spirit, about the selfish relief of dying before those we love, and I slipped it under my pillow so I could listen all night to the eternal voice that rises from the page like a secret murmured in my ear.

The next day I dared to look Marilou in the eyes and tell her: "Your poems are a thousand times better than mine." She turned red, as though a wish had been granted, and I apologized for having a heart that beats so powerfully for her.

Tacked to the wall next to my bed, another of Marilou's poems talks about butterflies that die in a stream, which are hopes swept away with the dead leaves, all the hopes of a happy life that we see disappear in the maelstrom of an unexpected tragedy. Reading it, you have such a keen sense of it you know the author has experienced it to the marrow of her bones. The nurses read it as they go by but they're not quite sure what to say about it or even perhaps what to think, seeing as how it's a tragic poem that wrenches you out of yourself and flings you directly into the invisible world of pain and anguish.

Once Marilou told me: "I've got a good thing for never being wrong: I close my eyes and let my mind go wherever it wants. I become a meadow full of flowers where my spirit is the wind."

I know it's sentimental, but it's sincere, and that's worth a lot.

Another time, Marilou confided to me that her father is an alcoholic, but that she doesn't see it as a problem.

"When he's been drinking, my father is as nice as anybody could want, funny and affectionate and not the slightest bit vulgar—even something of a poet—and I think he's happy, though everybody else—his boss, our neighbours, my mother, the family—gets upset. I don't want my father to change, though, because when he's sober, he's depressed and pitiful, so I don't want him to stop drinking."

At night, before I go to sleep I think about Marilou and about the truths that burst from deep inside her and beat against the doors of her mouth. It's hard to believe, but it's as if the sun is talking directly into the whites of my eyes.

Between her life and her loves,
she chooses to lose
her life.

I called home and my mother's going to come with my grandmother Langlois, my father's mother, the wife of the grandfather whose heart exploded, that I never knew. But I don't expect them for another hour or two, given that my mother has to pick up my grandmother in Sainte-Rose.

To keep my mind busy while the hourglass is draining I decide to write my letter from Purgatory for my grandmother Langlois. Yes, a letter from Purgatory. It's a secret project I've been nurturing, one that will make quite an impression in due course. As soon as I have a little time and I'm not feeling too bad, I go into hiding and write a letter to each of the people I love, and when I've finished, I'll tie them together and give the whole package to a friend, most likely my little saint Louis if he continues to get along so well, or maybe to my little saint Marilou if she emerges alive from her quicksand, and whichever one it is will have to mail all those letters one year after I die, on the anniversary of the event, and it will be like news from me arriving direct from Heaven. I've already written six, one to each of my parents, my sister, my brother, and my Baillargeon grandparents and today, it's my grandmother Langlois who flows from my hand and spreads across the paper.

Dear Grandma Émilia,

I hope you're well and that your arthritis isn't twisting your fingers too much. If the pain gets to be unbearable, I suggest that you have a wasp sting you every morning: apparently the venom relieves the pain of arthritis, yes, that's something I learned in the hospital.

Here in Purgatory I think about you every day (do you know that I still wear your Phentex slippers?), but that's just a manner of speaking, given that here there is neither

day nor night, only a kind of eternity that goes by quickly.
Do you remember the money you gave the diocese for
the souls in Purgatory? Well, it was used to redecorate and
to fix the leaky roof, anyway there's talk of enlarging it in
anticipation of a third world war or an epidemic. Purgatory is more modern than it used to be, but we're com-
fortable and the floor is always warm because Hell is right
underneath, but the noise bothers me a little, because of all
the rowdy parties at the devil's place down below.

It's already a year of life on earth since I left you for
Purgatory, where I've made some friends because there are
a lot of young people here, lots of third-world children.
My best pal comes from Bangladesh where he was an
Olympic athlete, a triple skipping champion (he used to
skip breakfast, lunch, and dinner every day). Luckily, he's
finally free from the agony of hunger, given that here we
live on spiritual nourishment, which is very practical. No
cooking, no dishwashing, no trouble. And because I was as
good as gold and I've been thoroughly purged of all the
filth I brought from my filthy life as a man, I leave here
tomorrow. I've seen Grandpa Langlois through the window and he's waiting to show me around Paradise. That
gave me a shock, since I'd never seen him before except in
photos. I laughed: he's shorter than I'd imagined, but he

seems to be in good shape with his red cheeks and bright eyes. The thing I found strangest here at first was not hearing my heart beat. It seems weird, we aren't used to it. We think that something's going badly, we worry, we panic, and then the old people reassure us, explain that it's normal and we calm down and breathe through our noses. But even if we no longer have a heart we can still love, and in fact I've met a girl, a beautiful drowning victim who . . .

All at once two images come through the door, images that are alive: my mother and my grandmother Langlois! My eyes bulge out of my skull and it takes my breath away, but my instinctive reaction is to hide my things under my pillow as fast as I can.

"Hello pet, how are you feeling today?"

How I'm feeling is, it could be better, could be worse, I'm struggling along, but I say that I feel okay. I kiss my grandmother and my mother, who haven't noticed what I was up to. I'm still a little petrified at being taken by surprised in the middle of Purgatory but I put my eyes back where they belong, shake my thumbs, and return to the world.

"Here, pet, here's some licorice and some chocolate."

It's the right kind of licorice too, nice and soft, cherry-flavored, and a big KitKat bar which I'm crazy about.

Grandma, you're so nice to me, I wonder how nice I am to you, anyway I haven't seen you for so long I've forgotten the day and time and I've practically forgotten the good taste, but here you are and for the time being you're my present. You are the hour, you're the day, and Mama and you are the second of life that is passing, that I'd like to hold onto for eternity. You are the blood that flows in my arteries, my heartbeats that count backwards as I watch out of the corner of my eyes, and I catch sight of the end of the world. You're beautiful, Grandma, dressed in your Sunday best although it's Tuesday, you're ankle-high to a grasshopper with your little comma curls, with your shining olive eyes, with the brooch on your blouse and the miniature incense burners that swing from the lobes of your ears. You smell good like an old-fashioned perfume, the essence of I don't know what old-fashioned flower, a daffodil maybe or a carnation or a dahlia, and you've always made me think of a saint with your devotion that is never-ending and your confidence in the invisible that always arrives tomorrow, leap-frogging over my nights.

Oh, Grandma, I would have loved to be a pure believer like you, and to grow up in the faith: to believe in an impetus that's unending all the way to the beyond, with no fear of the void and the unknown: dying would have been so much easier, but the nail could never be rammed into my big pig's head and I don't know why—maybe because of my goddamn impudence. In spite of all my attempts at good will, I've never felt the effects of the angels' goodness or Christ's love or God's mercy, and I insist on apologizing at your knees, but I'm painfully aware of the loneliness of night and the despair of lost souls.

To me, Grandma, your God is a poor lunatic who invented a son condemned to stagnate in the helplessness of child-hood, then be reborn eternally in the golden straw that we take to be rays of hope. What's worst is that this arrogant God apparently had the superhuman strength to live without being loved, and could have given humankind their true freedom by preventing them from being born, from suffer-ing, and from counting the years, but idly, he never found anything better to do than create beings he could put to the test by torturing them, then take back their martyred remains. A God who was truly good, truly almighty, would have had the courage to beget a man who bore no resem-blance to him, but our God wanted to have his own way, without trying to find out what people wanted. It's easy to see that he doesn't know us, that he's never been a lonely, unfortunate man. But that's nothing, nothing, it must be me who understands nothing, as usual, and it's you I love more than everything, Grandma Émilia, I love you more than God who's of no importance, and I thank you for being the only one who understands my passion, who always asks to read my poems even if you think they're of no interest whatsoever. The others don't give a damn and you feel sorry for me because, you say, I was born in a country of imbeciles who are satisfied too easily. You must know the country better than I do, you've been going to Mass there for so many years, and I don't dare contradict your ancient knowledge, but that's never stopped me from filling pages with Oh's and Ah's, or from writing *encor* for again without its silent *e* at the end. I've never waited for anyone to confuse me with someone else, I can do that on my own.

"That's a very fine poem on your wall . . . Who is Marilou D?"

"A girl I know."

I didn't dare tell her she's an Abenaki who has genocide in her blood and is stuffed with busulfan to the eyeballs.

"The icy water that . . . anxious to go and die . . . take away with the leaves . . . . all hope of rejuvenation . . . My goodness, that's sad . . ."

At which point we are interrupted by screams in the corridor, by a hell of a disturbance that makes us turn our heads. Friends rush to find out what's happening and come back with a mouth full of stinging scandal. We learn that a boy in room sixteen rang for the nurses to show them his claw-like, swollen penis that looks as if it's about to break away from his pelvic area, through putrefaction. Panic on the floor, urgent call for a doctor, then a sudden turn of events: the doctor discovers that the boy had slipped some Cracker Jack under his foreskin—three big pieces of caramel-coated pop-corn. Goodness! All around us, we hear people say that it's simply not done, that kind of tasteless joke, "out of respect for the truly sick," and the doctor and the nurses look indignant, as do my mother and my grandmother, and the only ones who have a good laugh are the rest of us, the truly sick.

Speaking of foreskins, I read somewhere about an old saint, Catherine of something or other, who claimed that she wore Christ's ring on her finger, the circle of flesh from his circumcision, and that today we can gaze upon the foreskin of baby Jesus in some European church; or drops of the Blessed Virgin's milk; lepers' scabs; pieces of the true Cross; five or six crowns of thorns; hairs from Noah's beard; a finger of St. John the Baptist at Saint-Jean-du-Doigt; the coins that were rammed into the eyes of Jesus on the Deposition from the Cross; even that there is a nail from the crucifixion in the crown of the kings of Italy. If I'd been lucky enough to live, I would have taken long trips to visit all those amazing churches that say absolutely nothing about God but everything about man, which is amazing in a different way.

"Here, pet, I hope you'll like this."

My eyes bulge at the sight of a generosity I wasn't expecting, that gives me unprecedented pleasure, that renders me speechless as it drops into my hands. My grandmother Émilia presents me with an extraordinary gift: a wonderful thick dictionary jam-packed with academic words to help me write flawless poems. To thank her as much as I can with my modest means, I promise to dedicate my work to her if I finish it in time for my funeral.

This afternoon I hoisted myself into my chrome-plated limousine to pay a visit to Louis at snack time.

"You smell funny today. Like eucalyptus, or turpentine."

"That's from the camphorated oil they rub me with," he said. "It's a tonic for the heart."

"How about that! I always thought tonic was something you drink with gin . . ."

Then, after some more gossip, Louis told me that the now-famous guy with the Cracker Jack has cancer of the lymph nodes, but that he fools around as if all he had was hay fever—but they don't know if he's being heroic or reckless.

The pudding and butter cookies arrived and we snacked together, talking about life like a pair of armchair philosophers sitting around a bed-table.

All at once, taking advantage of our moment of privacy, Louis decided to show me his chest, and it made a huge impression on me. Sporting a milk mustache, I sat and stared for a long time at Louis's pajama top open on the incredible purple, puffy seam that scored his chest from throat to stomach.

"Holy shit!" I said in admiration. "You look like Hollywood special effects!"

It's quite a sight and frankly, it suits him very well. I have a hunch that he'll impress quite a few girls with that Herculean scar of his. I, with my modest iliac tear, am a sorry sight next to the tremendous zipper that seems to be watching all on its own over the tremendous mystery of the Sacred Heart pierced with thorns, but hang on: I've got lots more to say about that.

When Louis had buttoned up, I asked him if he'd been afraid that he'd bite the dust on the pool table and he said no with a little shrug that commanded respect.

"You shouldn't worry about it," he told me. "You've just got two possibilities: either there is something, or there isn't. If there is something, that's good, because I've never killed anyone and I imagine it's a kind of paradise. But if there's nothing, pffft! I won't be around to see it . . ."

I smiled because of the pffft! which shows that you can die with your nose in the stars, as if that tragedy didn't concern us—which must stun the cowards and rejoice the hearts of others—and I decided to keep those good words of Louis's on ice, perhaps to exhale them when my breathing stops, in my final death rattle, at the twilight of existence.

Did I mention that Louis is a handsome blond? That's right, a handsome blond who makes girls swoon, the snake. Oh, I'm not jealous: it's an observation, that's all, but . . . I admit it, I feel a twinge. People are most handsome when they don't know it, that's understood, and when you know that you are, you're already a lot less handsome, but Louis doesn't know himself very well, and that weakness makes him invincible.

If the Eternal had let me choose a being in whom to live, I would have liked to live with the features of my friend Louis, to don his skin like a mantle, to try on his face like a balaclava, and his blond hair like a wig, to try out his voice and his hearing, to touch things with his fingers and look at the world through his blue eyes. The girls pamper him, the little skunk; he could thumb his nose at ugly billionaires, but that's not his style: his dignity gives him a rainbow as a halo.

He's smarter than I am too, I can't deny it. Once, with just a pencil and paper, he explained to me how Eratosthenes, a Greek mathematician from before Jesus Christ, had measured the earth's circumference thanks to the sun, which shed light on the bottom of a well in Egypt, and on some geometric equations; frankly, that amazed the socks off me.

Louis says that he doesn't know what he'll do later on; he's hesitating between paleontology, music, and bee-keeping like his grandfather. Yes, he's interested in Stegosaurus, in pterodactyls, and in Baluchiterium; apparently he can play caprices and bourrées; and he knows about royal jelly and the prodigious dance of the bees that execute skillful figures to show other pollen gatherers where to find the flowers.

Once, Louis told me that religious believers, many of whom hate science because it has ripped to shreds their perplexing stories, such as the fable of Adam and Eve, maintain that it was God himself who hid the fossils in the earth, to test the faith of geologists. Pffft! That's the stupidest thing I've ever heard. But it made me want to talk a little about evolution.

"You know about fossils," I said, "I'm sure you can answer a question I've been wondering about for ages."

"What's that?"

"Well . . . They say that man descended from an ape, but if that's true, how come there are still monkeys?"

"Because it isn't that man descends from an ape: man and monkey both descend from a common ancestor that isn't around any more. Monkeys and we are more like cousins who had the same great grandfather."

I knew perfectly well that he knew that, the little genius. He knows everything, everything except what will become of him, but the great mad dream of his life would have been to drive caravans along the silk route between China and Turkey, to trade in incense, Himalayan orchids, Karakorum rubies, and tigers' gall bladders; but there's a hitch: the profession hasn't existed for seven hundred years. Louis was born too late for the caravans, but just in time for something else, something he doesn't know yet, which means that he'll have a full life and that one day he'll be old and die because of his heart; and lots of people will cry at his funeral because his death will have been a major loss, on the same scale as the burning of books or the extinction of whales. I like saying that I've been his friend for ages because it gives me some artificial importance that I don't have in my everyday life.

> *The whales die away,*
> *but their oil lights up the night*
> *and the bedrooms of children*
> *who read wonderful books*

that tell of
the lost song of the whales.

Louis's room smells nicely of healing and you slip into it as into a flower in May, into a bell of lily-of-the-valley, with a smile on your lips, whereas my room reeks of suffering and disenchantment, and no one likes to step into that kind of rotten cabbage with a long face. It's as if the air inside my four walls doesn't sparkle like the air in my friend's room, that the light here doesn't have the same brightness as his hair, and anyway, the objects don't hear the same words.

I think that healing is an art and that you need to have a vocation, to have been touched by a fairy's magic wand, but I don't have the talent for that kind of broad-scale miracle. You might think that I'm defeatist and resigned, like my father, and that my true destiny has always been hidden in those deficits; that until today I'd never seen the young man that I am, because it's through ordeals that we really come into the world. I finally understand, in the light of the sky that has collapsed on me, that there's nothing exceptional about me and that I was defeated in advance. The only chance I've got now would be to beat the disease by a nose at the finish line so that I'd die of old age before his eyes, but I have to get a move on if I want to grow old in time. I'll have to move fast, cut corners, take shortcuts. Let's tie on our hats with wire: it's liable to be a descent into hell.

■

When I straighten up in my bed, I can see through the dirty window in my bachelor pad the city streets that will end their days in the grey St. Lawrence that flows in the distance beneath its grimy sky.

In the afternoon, we sometimes play at being a ship in distress on the St. Lawrence, to forget that we're in distress on earth: it shifts the pain. Yesterday we were still five ship's apprentices on board, but this morning we're only four: bad luck took away Benoît, the tall curly-headed boy who'd been with us for just a few days, and now we don't know if luck will bring him back some day or in what condition.

On the day he arrived, Benoît didn't seem very sick and we even wondered what he was doing here; he himself seemed to be floating like a cloud, but last night we got the picture when in the corridor, he vomited the three meals he'd eaten. The poor guy panicked, didn't know what was going on, and the vomit kept gushing non-stop, like lava from a volcano, even spattering the walls. The nurses yelled at him to go into a room, any room, so he could empty his guts into a toilet, and Benoît pushed open the door to the room of little

Magdalena, the Romanian girl whom the Romanians shipped here with a phony certificate that denied her hepatitis.

Unfortunately things took a turn for the worse: seeing as how Benoît couldn't keep anything down, they hooked him up to an IV and he spent the night moaning, then fell into the sea, into a coma, and this morning his messy bed was as empty as a ghost ship. If Benoît spends too long down in those depths, our budding friendship might suffer from it and we'll never see one another again.

During his first night with us, Benoît hadn't slept because he was so agitated, and he and I had taken advantage of our shared insomnia to fraternize sotto voce from one bed to the other.

"How come you ended up here?"

"I came down with cancer of the hipbone and it was like some stupid hamster at first, but now it's turning into an octopus. At night the nurses tie me to my bed because if I fell out in my sleep I'd break into smithereens like some cheap souvenir, or I'd hemorrhage because of the cyclophosphamide. I'm so brittle that my doctor calls me his china boy. He's okay, my personal doctor; doesn't say much but doesn't lie either, and I like that. Men like him get called oncologists and it's funny, but that word makes me think about soft caramels."

"Does it hurt being eaten away from inside?"

"Yes, but I pretend it doesn't. I hold everything back. We aren't babies any more, we can't regurgitate everything."

"Is it contagious?"

"No, don't worry, it's a private disease. It's related to your personality, it's in the marrow. But you're pretty sick yourself, aren't you? After all, God can't send you two fatal diseases!"

"I don't know if it's a disease, but I piss blood."

"Fuck! Do you know if you're going to piss it all away till you run out of blood and die?"

"I don't know, I don't think so. They told my mother I'd need two pairs of pjs. That must mean I'm going to live, doesn't it? Otherwise why two pairs?"

I hadn't said anything so I wouldn't demoralize him, but I'd already seen a bunch of young people go to the graveyard with all their stuff in a bag: pajamas, transistor, comics, games, magazines, colored pencils . . . Real little pharaohs.

> *I dreamed of being the Great Pyramid,*
> *invincible and eternal,*
> *but I am a porcelain garden*
> *under a shower of meteorites.*

The next day, I brought Benoît to Marilou's room to play that great game about the best last words. Our friend was only feeling so-so, but she still wanted to play with us because it's best to know beforehand. We clowned around with Benoît, we used words as long as your leg, the words of philosophers who think they know everything but haven't come anywhere near dying. We said that the essence of life is this, the essence of life is that, and so on and so forth, then we'd burst out laughing like little kids. We had so much imagination we decided to have a competition, a real, genuine competition, with paper and pencils: the first ever world championship of last words. In the end, thanks to her brilliant image, it was the lovely Marilou who took the prize.

The essence of life is vanilla.

Oh my Rilou of the gardens of my end of the world, I've changed my mind: in the end I wanted to be loved, but only by you. You see, I have a weakness for you, Marilou, I have even more, a lot more: I have a human pain and I'd give my life for you if I had one. Often, I imagine that you're my wife and melancholy stabs a hole into my heart, like the one in Louis's first heart, except that I'm well aware that I won't die at an old enough age to know about healing and love. You can't have everything.

Later, magically, my mother appeared while I was silently observing the nurse who'd come to empty the drawer and make the bed that Benoît had abandoned when he went away into a coma.

Oh no, Mama, you aren't disturbing me, you never disturb me. I wasn't doing anything: only thinking. I tell her that I'm tired and in the mood to not like anyone today, that anyone else, I'd tell to come back another time, but with her it's different. I come from her directly from heaven, as if it were a tunnel inside her, and she has all ancestral rights over me; what I like though is that she never aspires to be a godsend.

"First of all, don't move too much, darling, get some rest. I'm going to sit down and read for a while, I've brought a book."

She hugs me, but not too hard, so she won't pulverize me. Her mouth smells of dirty ashtray and I must smell of the end.

"How are Charlotte and Bruno?"

"They're fine . . . They want to come and see you . . . Saturday . . ."

She has a hard time finishing her sentence because a piece of life got stuck in her gullet, and then all of a sudden, it's strange, but I think about her womb where I spent nine months in water as salty as the ocean, a little like being in a coma maybe, and I really can't believe it. Oh Mama, please Mama, tell me that my life is a nightmare and that I'll wake up soon; either that or kill me with your own hands, then go and kill Charlotte and Bruno while there's still time, while they're still stunned with innocence and drugged with childhood, but I beg you, don't wait until they awaken to knowledge of the world and it's too late.

Little brother, little sister, I think about you often when I'm not asleep at midnight, and I catch a glimpse of you next to me in your night clothes. Charlotte, my little imp who instead of saying mashed potatoes, her favorite food, used to talk about *masked* potatoes; and Bruno, my little mischief-maker, who thought for a long time that his penis was a genius. I see you splashing around in Missisquoi Bay, fishing for minnows with a colander: I see the two of you in your ski-doo outfits with a frost-covered scarf just below your little mouths, sucking on lumps of ice off the thumbs of your mittens. I see you when the teeth missing from your gaping smiles made you lisp. Charlotte of the perpetual cold, I'll see you for all eternity with the pout that made you look like a little sick countess, and the golden snot from your over-stuffed nose. And I can't forget my tender-hearted Bruno who wanted so badly to console the weeping willows, who took a garden spade to peel porcupines squashed by cars off the pavement and buried them in a secret graveyard along the Rivière aux Brochets; my Bruno with the chocolate-colored eyes who always left room in his bed, and half a pillow, for his guardian angel.

But the most wonderful memory of you that I'll take away is of a night in July at the cottage. It was the eve of papa's birthday: it fell on a Sunday that year, which was convenient because papa only joined us at the cottage on Sunday mornings. It was midnight and the wind was playing in the leaves and gently stirring the curtains through the screens. You thought that mama and I were asleep but I had my eyes open in the dark and I heard you two get up on tiptoe. You were whispering secrets, then you went outside and I followed you in silence but accompanied by the crickets' song. When I saw you at the end of the gravel road, climbing our big poplar tree, so big that in the fall its tip scratched the bellies of migrating birds (that's the lie I made up to dazzle you) and suddenly I realized what dream you were chasing: you wanted to catch the moon and give it to papa for his birthday, the moon that seemed to be hanging like a wasps' nest from the high branches of the poplar, and I let you climb to the top, into the leaves turned silver by the moon. After a while, you came back down from the heights, crying, without the moon, and when your feet touched the ground you'd left one image of the world to enter a new one, where nothing would be as before, even though it was a beautiful summer night like so many others, near an old chalet under the trees. Ever since that memory came back to me, everything has been moving away from me as if I were scaring life, but what I'm fighting is to keep the taste of things in my mouth.

You've grown since that far-off night in July, you're no longer babies, that's understood, and I have to get used to looking at you differently, but every day that passes is a wound that's added to the others and reminds me of the seasons I used to know, I see them all and wish so much that I could get back the miraculous insouciance of that time. I remember as if it were yesterday: spring is a child who dreams and thinks he's a cloud, that's a favor; and autumn with its melancholy hours is like our memories; and summer is a thought filled with our feelings for the world, a light that catches us and elevates us; but only winter has a weight, winter is frighteningly heavy and it crushes us a little more each year, as if it wanted to kill us.

Mama, I'm afraid of dying in the winter and I hope that I'll make it till spring, and in the spring I'll want to be around till summer, and I think I'm actually not as brave as I thought. I want and I don't want, I understand everything and I understand nothing, I'm totally lost. I know that I could make all the malicious remarks that come into my head and make my mother cry, that everything would be forgiven in advance; and I know that after I die she would make me more attractive and that all the same, we would be happy in eternity, but I'm killing myself as I try to stifle all that furor inside me and I do everything I can to stop myself from hurting my mother the way I need so badly to hurt someone, in order to liberate all the violence and rancor that are brewing in my thoughts and seeking their revenge.

Life teaches me that it's infinitely easier to do harm than good, but I've sworn that I will be to the end a man who's worthy of the name, which means that as far as my mother is concerned, I'm a treasure. But I'm silently afraid and I don't sleep well at night and when morning comes I wish that I could sleep to avoid the light that throws me into a panic, but this is a communist country, blinds open, everyone up, six o'clock, everyone eats, even if no one is hungry, TV off, everyone to bed, and we simply follow the course of the sun, like a herd of animals.

One day I talked to my psychotherapist about it, in the hope that she'd finally be of some use. I explained to her that people are afraid of the dark but shouldn't be, because it's the light that is the source and the cause of all known ills. If there were nothing but night on Earth, people would be blind and lost and would fear going even farther astray in the darkness, but they wouldn't know that they're not all alike, because they would constantly be touching only those who are like them— beings with hands, shoulders, faces. Without light, people would take one another by the arm and advance slowly, all of them groping their way, taking the same hesitant steps, like brothers; no one would have any certainties and there would be no beliefs in their heads, but alas, the sun exists and people prefer to believe the lies of the light that makes them so unhappy.

Maryse Bouthillier can claim to understand me if she wants, I have my doubts; maybe it's because she claims that there's nothing she can do for me where that's concerned, seeing as how it's at night that we sleep and daytime when we open our eyes, that we can't turn a hospital upside down for one young man who wants to live the opposite way to everyone else, and it was because of that discord that our fragile love affair showed its first scratches.

"Martin, Stéphane, Patrick ... They phone me practically every day. They absolutely want to come and see you."

"Mama, I've told you a hundred times. I don't want anybody to see me."

"But they're your best friends!"

She doesn't realize that the last time I saw them, I saw them for the last time. You see, I couldn't stand to have them look at me as I am now, worse than naked, worse than dead, worse than eaten alive, in a way that they'd never seen me.

"Don't hassle me about it, Mama . . . I don't need to be seen or loved or consoled—especially not by my best friends."

I see my mother frowning sadly, shaken by my callousness, but she'll have to get used to it: this is just the beginning of my end and I intend to be tougher than life.

A moment later she finally admits that she doesn't understand me and I'm sorry, but I don't need to be understood now either.

"I want my friends to remember me as a living person."

Here I am all at once with no pity for my mother, but I don't have time now to don the white gloves of a princess so I won't hurt anyone's feelings: I may not look like much but I'm somewhere else now; I'm not bragging, I am inside my truth that emerges naked and aching from the well, that flays the ears and feelings of others till they bleed.

I may be unfair and a bastard but I'm the dead man: I'm the one who makes all the decisions, to the end. It's my turn to dictate my umpteen wishes and anyone who doesn't like it can just steal a corpse from a morgue and perform their mystical experiments and say their shitty prayers over it. I don't feel like giving them a chance to show the crowd how sensitive they are. They can wait for an accident to happen at the corner of the boulevard if they want to make a spectacle of themselves. As for me, I've shut down the theatre for good and swallowed the key.

All is dark, good night. We'll meet again some frosty Friday in July.

■

One early morning came the great day for Louis, who went back to live in the world of the living where he may become a fossil hunter, a violinist, or a beekeeper in the country like his grandfather Élohim, Élohim Vézina. But paleontology or music, it's all the same: both mean reinventing vanished worlds; and if he goes into honey, he'll transform workers into queens, which amounts to creating impossible worlds. Whatever Louis does, his life will be a dazzling success, I can sense it, and when I saw him rushing into the elevator with his parents, some warmth left my life and I swallowed a draft that went down the wrong way on an early morning that was a great day. The last image: Louis is standing between his misty-eyed parents, parents happy to be finally taking their child home where a mountain of presents awaits, and the light from the fluorescent fixtures gleams in the eyes of my friend like frozen lightning: my friend whose last trauma-tized gaze locks with mine.

I remember thinking: "When I die, maybe the universe all around me will fade into the night and I'll stay behind alone, like a star without a sky."

At which point I drove slowly to my bachelor pad where I listened to some music on the radio.

That afternoon, to dispel my boredom, I ran a fever.

> *I think about a million mysteries*
> *with mercury under my tongue,*
> *and I wonder:*
> *if I were to bite the thermometer,*
> *and if I were to drink mercurochrome,*
> *would I see the other side of worlds?*

I would have liked to go on writing stupid poems, even to make a silly career of it, why not? You need to find some way to get your daily bread and to make yourself loved, if you want to die old and popular. And then one day I made the most amazing discovery in my new dictionary: I read that during the eighteenth century, there lived in Vienna an Italian poet named Metastasio: unbelievable but true. Pietro Trapassi, known as Metastasio, or Pierre Metastasis, so I decided then and there to adopt his nutty pseudonym, and I became the poet Metastasio, king of the hospital. I knew that with a name like that I could have earned my daily bread and even more, even a cosy little life, and maybe Marilou would have agreed to marry a poet, even a shitty poet, what's the harm in that?

She could have taught me how to be intelligent; I would have been a better poet and a better husband, anyway I finally would have understood that poetry is a dirty trick and I would have finally stopped writing. And then we could have had children who weren't too idiotic, but who would have thought that they were even more so, like all children. I think I would have been a strange father, with a punitive foot but a helping hand, a father with two faces, like the moon that streaks the night: at least I admit it. I wouldn't have chained myself to my children's bedsides, and I wouldn't have tickled them half to death, that's not my idea of the ideal life, but I would have watched over them secretly from deep inside my silence, and when they turned thirty, they would have understood everything, and finally, they would have loved me. I would have educated them the hard way, cared for them and cuddled them in the proper time and place, I'd have washed and fed them but above all, I'd have lied to them superbly, I'd have stuffed them with fables all the way to the uvula; I would have exhausted like nobody else treasure troves of unscrupulous tricks to make them love the world. You have to lie to children, you see, constantly, like breathing, day after day and even at night, when they dream, you have to pour beautiful lies into their ears to intoxicate them, delude them, in a world of sugar and honey and music. If not, unless you have that tremendous courage, you have to strangle them with the umbilical cord at birth, or drown them in the bathtub, give them a hemlock cocktail, sacrifice them in a bed of flames, surrounded by their dolls and toys. Force-fed on lies that way, our children in turn would have written poems one night, to give themselves the illusion that they're not too stupid, then they'd have married someone better than them who would have taught them the deep, essential truths about themselves, and they'd have stopped writing thanks to that luminous love. And the snake would have eaten its tail. Words, silence, words, silence, words, silence . . . To be born and die and born and die, ad infinitum. Lives are idiots: they only know how to make loops, like comets or yoyos, but nothing better has yet been found.

I talk, I talk, and I don't even dream any more. Am I in despair? I think I'm quite simply sincere, and that can be fatal.

> *Wise men and fools*
> *don't have the same life,*
> *but do they share the same death?*
> *And why*
> *this strange need*
> *to believe that one's been created by a god?*
> *What harm would there be*
> *if one were born from the rain?*

Yes, I know, you have to be very sincere to spew such whining, but I would rather be sincere than hypocritical, because hypocrites learn all there is to know about whining, and they spend their lives not repeating them so that they'll seem intelligent, but hypocrites are no smarter than whiners: just better educated.

It's Saturday, lazy day but feast of nothing.

Outside, it's raining windows full of dirty November rain, as if the throats of the clouds had been slit. In the sky, monstrous fumes are rolling, crushers of birds and of dead leaves yanked off drowsy trees; the wind is fragrant with the end of time and I shiver and the sound of the rain makes me want to urinate all the time. Mind you I drink a gallon of water per day, I have to, so that the cyclophosphamide won't wreck my kidneys, which would make me piss blood like Benoît.

Speaking of blood, I was surprised to see the famous Cracker Jack boy turn up in my room yesterday. He'd heard about my poems from his favourite nurse and wanted to have a look at me. His name is Gaétan and he doesn't look the least bit stupid. Frankly, it's hard to imagine him stuffing popcorn under his foreskin, but that's part of his charm. We talked cuisine and nitrogenous mustard, like gourmets. He, Gaétan, is a real mulligatawny stew, which he savors along with doxorubicin, bleomycin, vinblastine, and dacarbazine, and his gums hemorrhaged the other night when he was brushing his teeth. He admitted that time passes very slowly, that he's sick of being sick, and we promised to get together again to boost one another's morale. Which reminded me that ever since I've been condemned to be nothing but what I am, I too think about time as it passes or doesn't pass, depending on the time of day, or the feelings that haunt us. Faced with cruel time only saints have the superhuman strength to be constantly equal to themselves, while little pagans like me are uncertain and frail: life breaks us and we don't know how to hold onto our youth and our faith. Anyway, there's one thing I've noticed: it's often at night, when no one can see us, that we grow old. In the day-time, the blows send us reeling, but at night we forgive them for everything in exchange for a little fat and nourishing old age. We like to think that it's the good thick soup of wisdom, but it's bribery. Those who understand the mechanics of life ape it and do everything the same way, handing out skimpy joys and random forms of happiness where required, just enough to entice the needy, who go on to lick the boots of destitution. Yes, life is unfair, that's its job: there will always be people to suffer agony, because happiness costs an arm and a leg and because there'll never be enough for every-one. It's written in the sky for anyone who can read: we will always be short of arms and legs.

My only piece of luck is that I'll have been a holy man, because saints are as strong as mountain rock, but I've always been afraid of saintliness because of perfection, which is not of this world, and because of the halo pins that you have to drive into your scalp.

This morning, I phoned Louis, in Mascouche, my little Saint Louis who is in perfect health: his heart which is sewn with gold thread follows the furious rhythm of a new life and is combing the countryside. Louis admitted that he misses me and I told him to go out and play hockey in the street, that it would pass. I'm bored too, but you have to know how to be silent, and you have to have the courage to be blunt; otherwise, otherwise a man can sink very low, to the point of pity which is at the bottom of the ladder of feelings.

I did not discover
the rings of Saturn
because I was looking elsewhere,
but I am discovering
the emptiness of the world
when I look at the space
occupied by you.

Benoît is feeling better now too: he's no longer in a coma pissing blood and he's come back to our room with some unbelievable memories of his long fainting spell, impressions that he recounts with flames in his eyes and there we are, open-mouthed with wonder, nearly envying him. He says that he saw angels, gods, naked women with the heads of vultures, unicorns of fire and geometrical figures that murmured secrets to him in a swirl of asteroids; that he was a giant and the next moment a midget; and that in the end he'd metamorphosed into an Easter Island statue burned by the sun and by albatross droppings; and then he heard all the prayers his parents had mumbled at his bedside and he had the impression that he was in a church where he was the Holy Ghost.

"I loved being in a coma, but I wouldn't go back there."

He brought back some gems of course, but still, he'd had the fright of his life, which makes for an expensive gem.

His doctor, who knows everything, told him that his name comes from the Latin, *beneeit*, which is the past participle of the verb "to bless." Benoît is very proud of that and keeps repeating that he is blessed by the gods, so much so that I think about changing his name to crown him Saint Benoît, then baptise him again with garlic and wine, like a king.

I asked him: "Did you keep my bed in ICU nice and warm?"

He laughed, but it was forced.

I like Benoît a lot: he's a sensitive guy who doesn't deserve to die right away and who has worked hard for his reprieve; I know that he'll make good use of his gift of days.

One night I secretly did something crazy: I addressed a prayer to him, a real one, a prayer from far away, from the darkness deep inside me, a prayer that rises up in the mist, in a breath of air that is seeking its light; I asked him to grant me recovery, yes, I asked that of Benoît, who possesses the mysterious key to it. And if some day I recover and I leave here as one piece of meat, standing on my own two feet with my good head intact on my shoulders, I vow in the presence of men that I will religiously follow my friend like a shadow and even better: I will follow him like a little Benedictine and I'll build chapels in his wake.

One morning, Benoît and I talked about school, about our friends who are becoming educated without us and are probably very learned now. I said: "I used to love geography; meteorite craters, the sea-bottoms, minerals, fairy chimneys. I would have loved to go down inside volcanoes, study earthquakes, prospect for oil in the Yukon and visit fabulous countries like Mozambique, Laos or Uruguay. Or maybe I'd have liked to be a goalie."

"If I ever get better," said Benoît, "I promise I'll find my way into the digestive tract or become a nephrologist . . . Yes, I'll do good to the kidneys of the entire world . . ."

I don't know why, but the nurses pour Benoît's urine into flasks on the windowsill in our room. It could be that they want to test its purity by daylight, but it embarrasses him. Everybody teases him to make him blush, but he takes it well: he isn't going to die, and he'll have his whole lifetime to forget this humiliation. In the meantime, the morning sun rises in Benoît's golden piss, through the glass flasks, and the light in our room is like the beautiful light from a stained-glass window.

As for little Magdalena who's betrayed by jaundice, she is still in the same room where she dozes in a stable condition, which is fantastic considering her liver. Her new court-assigned parents want to return her to sender in Romania because of a hidden defect that didn't appear on the contract they signed during the transaction with the vendors. While they wait for the verdict of the commercial court, they've got some new catalogues and they're going over some fresh mer-chandise from the child market. While Magdalena, all alone in her corner, dreams of the Black Sea and the Carpathians, unless someone else buys her, here or in another rich coun-try, or she becomes a ward of the state. To create a life for yourself out of wind is risky, but she has no choice: she's all alone in the world.

Speaking of creating your life, I have a new friend: Erik with a k but no accent, like Erik the Red, the famous Viking from the 1000s, bishop of Greenland and father of Leif, who came to America according to the history books.

My friend Erik has inherited a malformation that creates little pockets in his oesophagus where food accumulates and rots, so his breath stinks like a corpse. Because of those anomalies in his pipe, the poor guy chokes on his saliva and snot at night. It's no joke, but what I like about him is that he hates to talk about himself, like me about me, and we quickly became buddies who understand each other in secret, like the uvula and the epiglottis.

"I just have to not laugh too much."

When he laughs too much he coughs, but they'll figure out something.

"They're going to open my pharynx and go in and plug the pockets."

The other day, I was feeling better than usual and felt like having some fun, so I invited Erik to come with me and play in the elevator to check out the different floors. At one point he said to me: "I don't like fluorescent lights, the light they give is cold, like the light of the moon." I'd never thought about it, but he's got something there.

First, we looked for the nursery, because we were in the mood to see some newborns for a change in routine, but we were laughing like loons and my friend was coughing a lot—we were laughing because we felt as if we were going to the zoo. A patient attendant even reprimanded us: he thought we were having a little too much fun.

Along the way, we got lost in the maze of corridors and floors, then made our way to the very back of the hospital, to gynecology, where expressionless women were waiting on chairs along the grey walls under crackling fluorescent lights and everywhere, we had the impression that we were disturbing people, getting in the way of the doctors and nurses who were giving us dirty looks; so what we did was, we went downstairs and took a walk around the ground floor and watched the ambulances arrive, but that was depressing.

That was how we ended up in the lobby, where patients in hospital gowns go to smoke. A little lady, just skin and bones and tired-looking, dragging her IV, sat there in a diamond of sunlight and seemed lost in her cigarette smoke.

"These are my last ones," she said. "Tomorrow they're taking out my larynx. I'd like to keep it in a jar as a souvenir, like my gallstones, but they say no."

Her voice was full of scratches that made me want to clear my throat. When she found out what Erik and I had, she thought we were a little too young to be sick and she said it was really a pity and then she told us about her husband, whom she missed a lot.

"At the end, they poked a hole in his throat and I had to stick his cigarette in so he could smoke it . . ."

I thought to myself that my parents ought to stop smoking if they don't want to end up like that, all eaten up by cancer, when suddenly I noticed next to the lady a dishevelled gentleman in a bathrobe, who was listening to every word and nodding. The lady noticed and started to regard him out of the corner of her eye: the man caught her look and they ended up introducing themselves and yakking together.

"Ah those blasted specialists! They haven't got a brain between them!"

"They must have, Madame, or they wouldn't last very long."

"I wonder what there is in this serum that keeps us alive."

"Proteins, glucose, medication, things like that."

It was a nice thing to see, two old sick people who were becoming friends before our eyes.

"What about you, what brings you here?"

"My prostate."

Seeing that they were getting along just fine without us, we wished them a good day and successful surgeries, then we went and begged for pennies at the front door of the hospital, wanting to see which one of us would be a better beggar, but it wasn't fair, because my wheelchair automatically made me a sorrier sight than Erik.

We begged for five minutes, until a grouchy sentry chased us away, saying that just because we were sick it didn't mean that we could do whatever we felt like. Which wasn't wrong. We didn't push it, but went off to feed our money to the vending machines in the first basement that sold Coke and candy. I gave Erik a few coins so that we'd be fifty–fifty.

"Take this," I told him as a joke, "it's a tip for pushing my carcass all over in my coach."

Then, in front of an automatic coffee-maker, we had a little gab with a woman who told us she had a "utopic pregnancy." We thought to ourselves that she would give birth to a dream, poor thing, or to a stillborn hope. Needless to say, we didn't dare ask her where the nursery was; we wished her good luck and she disappeared with her miserable cardboard cup of coffee. Afterwards, in the cafeteria, we listened to a couple of comical patients who were going through the *Journal de Montréal* and at the same time talking about some doctors and their "Hypocrital Oath."

Before we went back to our bachelor pads, we got a fantastic idea: Erik pushed me to Abbé Guillemette's chapel in the chronics' wing. The good father of desperate causes had limped away somewhere else, as we'd hoped, so we had some fun: we desecrated the tabernacle. Each of us took a healthy swig of his sweet Hungarian wine, then we stole some missals and a handful of Hosts. Erik, a born looter, actually ripped off a beautiful gold tulip-shaped chalice to add to his personal collection of sacred objects—he'd already stolen a monstrance, an extreme unction kit and, one night, an episcopal ring from the bishop's palace in Saint-Jérôme, keeping all these jewels for the future woman in his life.

"To beg forgiveness for our sins," I said, "we'll come to Abbé Guillemette's mass on Sunday."

At that, Erik said he'd always thought it was atheism that kept him from swallowing the Host during communion, but it was just a malformation of the esophagus, and he was disappointed.

The next night, huddled under my sheets, I crunched some Christ-like vinegar chips by the light of my miniature flashlight, while I read my missal, and I saw that I'd been lucky: it was a special edition, a missal for subscribers to *Prions en l'Église* that was as thick as ten ordinary ones and crammed with texts, including Paul's first epistle to the Corinthians. At the end of chapter five was written in black and white: "But them that are without God judgeth. Therefore put away from among yourselves that wicked person." That sounded like a roundabout accusation and I wondered if everything is my fault. It's true: maybe it's because my poor old turnip only half-loves anything and that's what made it start to fall apart and rot. You see that in sons-of-bitches and cowards: they live, but they don't have a heart, and you tell yourself it doesn't make sense. I also learned that my body is a member of Christ and that by having sex, I would have

made it the member of a prostitute. Pffff! I've never read anything so wacky.

Finally, I don't like the epistles. I'm not wild about Saint
Paul either, he's neurotic. Anyway, I just don't like the Bible,
that People's Almanac with too much magic. To tell the
truth, I might have followed Christ if he'd thrown at me the
cure-all called a "miracle" that's so humiliating. For if a miracle is possible, why not miracles all the time, nothing but
miracles? Why not cure me? And why not eternal life on
earth rather than in heaven? I'm extremely fond of that star
which is the cradle of my days and the bed of my nights. The
sky should be decked out in all its finery if it wants me to
forget my dear planet Earth, but let me tell you quite frankly:
the sky is dreaming in Technicolor. Up there, eternity must
be never-ending.

Crunching my last sacred chip, I thought about the endless fields of wheat that had to be cut down to make all the
hosts that have been swallowed since communicants started
to criss-cross the universe, and I thought to myself that you
just have to repeat the same action again and again for it to
lose all its meaning. It's the same phenomenon that destroys
words. I've chewed my first name in my head much too
long: Fré-dé-ric, Fré-dé-ric, Fré-dé-ric; fifteen or twenty
times and I'd lost all my flavor, like an old wad of gum.

The next day, I told Benoît what I'd done and he didn't like the way I'd ripped off the Bible.

"My mother taught me that you must never take the words out of the Bible," Benoît told me. "You have to read it from far away, barely seeing it, to grasp the words and everything that surrounds them. You must try to see it whole, like a landscape or a painting, or the most important part of it escapes us. It's like when Jesus restored sight to the blind man in the gospel according to Matthew: you mustn't think that the blind man really has his sight restored! The blind man doesn't magically start to see the real sun in the real sky, does he? That would be too easy! He is still blind to the world of objects, but Jesus fills him with a new light that will keep him forever from getting lost in the night of his heart. The blind man who sees doesn't mean merely 'the blind man who sees,' it means 'the blind man who believes.' It's like when Jesus heals the paralytic in Capharnaum: the paralytic doesn't really get up from his bed, that would be too stupid, too cruel for any handicapped people who read the Bible; what Jesus did do was restore his dignity. Faith makes the paralytic grow to the height of other men and that is the true miracle. The proof that I'm right is that my mother has a paraplegic friend who never asked Heaven to send her a new pair of legs that can walk. She never engaged in blackmail like those who promise to build a niche for the Blessed Virgin outside their house if they obtain favors from Heaven. She believes in God just as she is, without disgracing herself, and her life is enough for her, and she has never refused that gift from God because faith, genuine faith, isn't about legs."

That amazed me all the way to Sunday, but I still ventured a remark.

"But . . . all those crutches hanging on the walls of St. Joseph's Oratory, what do they mean?"

"Not a thing. If you've noticed, there are just old-fashioned crutches from the olden days to make a period décor and attract tourists, to impress people who never read the Bible or who don't understand it."

That stopped me in my tracks And then the tireless Benoît made another thoughtful observation.

"The beauty of the Bible is that it's full of allegories."

Right. He's gone farther than the rest of us, my friend Benoît; what we know about allegories is limited to allegorical floats in parades. If it had come from any other seventeen-year-old, I'd have said: "He's too young to talk like that, he's just repeating something he heard his mother say." But since it had come from the mouth of my little saint Benoît, whom

I respect and who is a reliable source, I knew that his ideas must be of a very high quality. I promised myself that I'd think scrupulously about what he'd said and try to understand it all—while wondering if it was Benoît himself, the holy man I might have wanted to be but never would because of lack of time. The thing is, double lives are fine for the movies, but real everyday life isn't so generous: it doesn't give alms twice; and my dream life will be lived by another man who might well be Benoît himself, who knows?

The day after that theological discussion, I introduced Erik to Marilou, who doesn't look like an Abenaki any more: she's lost her hair because of her chemotherapy with busulfan, and she cries with her face hidden in her pillow. In the beauty test that pits her against the light of day, Marilou is losing ground. That light, which didn't come up to her ankle before, is now level with her navel. You could see her as an equinoctial tide rising higher and higher and threatening to submerge everything human about her. You might say that the daylight will conquer her just as, in the morning, it conquers the night, and that upsets me so much that it will be the death of me.

If my bone marrow had been good I would have wanted to graft myself to Marilou forever.

For now we see,
through a glass,
as a riddle
but then
it will be face to face.

It's all of Saint Paul that I've squeezed into that brief poem, like an evil genie in a bottle, to see how it would affect me, and frankly, it scares me, like his *O death, where is thy victory?* I wonder if survival in a world so false wouldn't be more horrifying than annihilation pure and simple, of which a premonition is already slitting my throat in my bed. Yes, I'm very afraid of this world of saints, priests, and prophets who live inhuman lives, this world that wants to tell us how to exist and how to see, but that doesn't even have the courage to be lucid, that loses track of us in its mirrors; and Saint Paul's world is an unhealthy world where the reversal of things spoils a man, where what I consider to be truth is evil and my impulses, sins—and it's that fake world that wants to destroy our hope for happiness in the present tense, to disturb us endlessly.

Those stupidities make me aggressive, and instead of the great face-to-face encounter announced by Saint Paul, I want to be ass-to-ass and even better face-to-ass: my ass in his face.

Fine, I knew it: word spread like wild horses all the way to high places and the powers that be don't like my new pseudonym at all, nor even the thought that I've anabaptised myself all alone in my corner, without telling them about my metamorphosis. I don't know, you could say that this symbolic mutation terrifies them more than any genetic mutation, and that they think I'm ripe for a brief stay in psychiatry, all expenses paid, but I tell them: I'm not just anybody, I am the poet Metastasio and I'm very well known in my family, even my father calls me by my first name and anyway, I'm in the dictionary, protected by an Austrian empress, queen of Bohemia and Hungary—but they're philistines. All they want is to cut off my balls in an emergency procedure because they're sick and tired of seeing me inseminate the world in my fashion. I disgust them by my way of being alive, my way of biting into death, the stars and God. Until my poor mother dissolves into tears because the abbé of desperate causes shouts down all the corridors that I've turned out badly and that I'm lost in revolt and selfishness; because the nurses and my oncologist think my relationship with disease is unhealthy; and because my psychotherapist talks about complacency in morbidity, or something along those lines that's trying to say something. Fuck! Can't a person die the way he wants here for Christ's sake? Do I waste my time telling *you* how to live? Do I have to jump off the seventh floor to tear myself away from your rabid claws?

One morning, they called on Maryse Bouthillier to pay an emergency visit to my bedside to worm some information out of me.

"Why did you pick that for a name? Do you realize how traumatic it could be for the people who love you and hope to see you cured? What are you trying to tell us anyway?"

Now listen up, sweetie, this is going to leave traces of fire in your educated brain: I am trying to tell you that happiness is not to be found in the bombast of eternity or in the promises of someone drunk on gods or demons, or in the emotional backwardness of those who can't live for a minute without swindling us with their shitty hope. Happiness and freedom I throw to the pigs: what I believe is that any man worthy of the name ought to give up his freedom and happiness and espouse the unhappiness of the lost; to experience the way they suffer like slaves in his very flesh; but also to recognize good even in the hotheads who deny themselves and don't believe in anything. Yes, you have to relinquish yourself and the world of objects in order to embrace ugliness, loneliness, old age, sickness and death—woes that make people better: humble and generous, human and merciful, attached to their peers and in love with their last days on earth. It's true. There's nothing like a slow death to convert with one stroke of a magic wand the toughest sons of bitches.

The blind eyes all around me may not see it, but I am more humble, more generous and more human than ever; however, my way of being human is so foreign to them that they see only inhumanity. We are born to not understand one another and it's pointless to go any farther.

All at once my crazy eyes are staring into the wide-open ones of my psychotherapist; to finish her off, I said: "It's like the business of the chicken and the egg; we don't know if it's hysteria or psychotherapy that appeared on earth first."

You might think that it drove her around the bend, and there are good reasons to smash the lead in her pencil along with the look in her eyes, because my poor shrink vanished into thin air and didn't leave a forwarding address.

Farewell, lovely guardian angel who loved so much to shovel pink clouds for me; we'll meet again some frosty Friday in July.

> *In the garden of prides,*
> *the jasmine wood*
> *perfumes the axe that strikes it,*

and the raspberry bush
bleeds to death
on the rubies it refuses to give up.

This morning I opened my eyes to see my grandmother Langlois stroking my hand and it moved me to tears, but I swallowed, choked, drowned them all. For days now, I've been so mean to everybody and I'm so ashamed of myself that I don't even know if I'm sincere, and when in doubt I do nowt, I nip in the bud any flowers of the truth, but my grandmother wasn't born yesterday and it won't be me who scares her and keeps her from approaching the abyss that is me.

"I was very touched by your story about the poet Metastasio," she whispered. "I'd like to help you, to make you happy, but you'll have to explain what you want, what you think, and why you've christened yourself with a new name—please . . ."

Grandma Émilia, you understand me better than I understand myself, and you make my icy heart melt into holy water, you make me more transparent than a winter sky, and if anyone will test my love of secrecy, it's you more than anyone else, and I would gladly open my mortal wound to you and reveal to you the mystery of my blood.

"That's because I want to see in the letters of my name the true letters of the end . . . And I'd like to know what a man whose very name signified Death might have written . . ."

My grandmother's beautiful green eyes run over my face and I feel warm at being loved and understood, and I'm so ashamed that I turn around abruptly to bury my face in the pillow.

"I'll find them for you, I'll find the books by that Italian poet of yours, sweetheart. I'll go to every bookstore in Montreal and you'll see, I'll bring you what you want."

You're too generous and too kind to me, Grandma, you're too amazing and you understand me too well; how can it be, I can't go on living like this, I'll never be able to look you in the eyes now that you know my secret, but Grandma, please forgive me, I beg your forgiveness for all the pain I've caused around me, for all the sorrow I cause for those who love me, but life is atrocious, and I change with the days, and you could say that I'm moving away from the world little by little, that I'm swept away like a cork, and that terrifies me. I no longer recognize myself and I'm haunted by a faceless shadow that comes and goes without a sound, that some-times moves aside to leave me with the illusion that I am causing myself to be forgotten, but the shadow of Satan always comes back down through the ceiling, and though I grit my teeth with all my might, though I'm scared silly, it comes back inside through my mouth and my backside, and when I wake up I see that I have not emerged unscathed, that I'm being eaten alive, as if the night that dwells in me when I sleep retreats from me in the morning, half carrying me away.

Yes, Grandma, it's appalling: every day I lose half of what I still possessed the day before, and every day after that I again lose half of the half, and so on, but I won't be able to waste away like that forever, and soon I'll bite the dust, stripped of my entire small capital, and I'll lie in the grass, my heart ripped out of my chest like a potato from the earth. What is most terrible is that this baleful shadow has no physical thickness, no carnal depth, but it's there all right, eating away like acid but as impossible to grasp as the wind, and you can feel it biting into the living flesh, you can feel it wandering inside you like a toxic cloud. *Fuck you!* I shout at it, at that mother-fucker, get the fuck away from me, you fucking shit! But I don't scare it with my altar boy's profanity, and I look like a piece of filth that's lost all dignity and doesn't know what to cling to or from whom to beg forgiveness, but no one can do anything, not you or the limping abbé or the icons of Christ, and I descend alone deep into the darkness, and it's starting to be real for real, it's no longer words or images, I can truly see the faces of my life being erased, I can see my beloved hands that want to keep me in the light moving away. And in the distance the sounds and the voices die away too and all I can hear inside my skull is the horrible bursting of metastases. My eyelids are closing for what may be the last time and I am consumed by icy fear and abandonment.

O Grandma Émilia, please let me kiss your bare feet and please, Grandma, please, bless me, bless me, I need it as badly as I need clean water and human warmth.

This morning I was completely lost when I opened my eyes onto the grey light spilling over all around the warped aluminum venetian blind, so demoralizing.

I had dreamed that my grandmother Émilia was still here with me and it destroyed me not to see her at my side. Anyway I can't really tell you why, but that light, which is a little dirty, a little chalky, seemed to me like the light of Sunday, and I was not mistaken: today is Sunday, again, it's Sunday everywhere you look, Sunday in every direction, in every corner of the hospital, and there's no escaping it. These days, every day seems like Sunday and I'm bored on that day.

Lying on my bed I have the impression that I'm floating in the salt of the Dead Sea. I look outside, not trying to see anything in particular, and my gaze is lost in the distance. What I could see I've already seen a thousand times and nothing interests me any more. I think about a phrase from the Bible that I'd read in my stolen missal: "A sound heart is the life of the flesh: but envy is the rottenness of the bones." Meaning that I envied someone something? . . . The lives of others, most likely; the sound heart of those who have no knowledge of what I know.

I sigh, but if I couldn't sigh it would amount to the same thing; even the stars would stay in the same place and the sun would trace its arc of fire in the firmament; and the moon, bride of the night, would lose some blood every month, as always.

Outside the winds are sobbing for no one and it's a waste of breath; and the December gusts are hurling snow and ice violently against the windowpanes. You might think they were whirlwinds of salt and the moans of a child, and tears blur my eyes when I think about how I've spent my life: I didn't realize how quickly I was in the process of losing everything; I didn't understand that every day that doesn't seem like much is one small cog in the great mechanism of universal loss.

It's strange, but ever since I was little I have wondered if there is a heaven in Heaven, and I finally found the answer in my missal, which was ill begotten but of which I've taken great advantage; it was in a passage in the Book of Kings where Solomon says, "Behold, the heaven and heaven of heavens cannot contain thee." Which is what I thought: death is an abyss.

Aside from that, it seems that priests wear a purple chasuble for the liturgy of the corpses. I think that's as vulgar as a necklace on a dog. Why not a green one like they wear on ordinary Sundays? Why not an apron like you wear in art class? Pj's? A kimono? A Maurice Richard jersey? And anyway, why get dressed to devour the body of Christ who died in the purity of his nakedness?

At noon I didn't eat much. I don't know, it's as if nothing has any taste. The only thing I can still eat is a raw potato now and then, a spud with salt. Still, I forced myself to drink my milk, to encourage my bones to do their job till the end of the week that's just starting, but I spat out everything else—the cold minced steak, the boiled-to-death beans, the raspberry Jell-O with its chignon of fake whipped cream. If my dog had been there he'd have had a feast, but as for me, every day I eat less than the day before. You could say that I'm losing hope.

Earlier that morning, some clowns came to horse around in our wing, because the healthy grownups decided that the young patients ought to laugh, even if it was for no good reason. They're retards, those healthy people: they think that laughter can cure! You can see that they've never suffered. As for me I didn't laugh once. Not because I'm more serious than the pope, but because the clowns were as dumb as they come. The dumbest member of the pack was called *Paztèque*, with a *z* as in *les zimbéciles* and the little clown wanted to fool around with my fragile poet's tools. I could see him coming, but I didn't have time to rip off one of his arms, and he managed to snap the lead on my favourite pencil, the one that writes my not-so-bad poems. I wanted to kill the shithead, but I'd have had to kill two of them: another penguin followed Paztèque, like a tail, a female clown this one, actually the fairy Électricité with holes in her teeth, a vulgar bundle of nerves who came rushing into the rooms to sneer and grope at all the IV bags. They're chimpanzees, totally cretinous. At this point, they could have at least arranged to let us have a smoke on the sly, or give us a beer, or hike up the nurses' skirts, something like that, adult things that would have really done us some good. Instead, they make us sick with their kitchy-kitchy koo-ing.

O misery! Even if you're old when you die you wouldn't have lived old, poor little babies.

Things were already going badly when out of the blue, here comes Abbé Guillemette like a shadow from a sepulchre to Christianize me at my bedside. I don't know why, but the churchman had got it into his bald head to forgive me for the sins in my life, if I understood him correctly, or maybe he wanted to anoint me with the olive oil he'd hidden in a vial under his robe, but I told him that I'd always refuse to do penance in front of him, and that I'll never allow anyone to grope me but myself or a woman.

Yes, perhaps I would have let myself be anointed by a female priest, out of gallantry or affection, but definitely not by a hospital priest to whom I owe nothing.

To each his sense of decency, and the dead will be sadly lamented.

"Fine, all right, you don't want to do penance, very well . . . but . . . could I at least know why?"

"Because I'm perfect."

Oh là là! That gaping Abbé must think I'm one hell of a comedian. You can see how frustrating it is for him to have landed on someone virtuous who outstrips him, and of course he doesn't want to believe me—this man who always sees himself floating above the flock—but a child of a monkey like him will never wear me down, I'm no patsy, I've been tempered by a naked flame, by cyclophosphamides and cobalt!

"Don't give me that, Frédéric, what you said makes no sense . . . Nobody's perfect . . ."

"I am! And I'm not stringing you a line, I'm no Comtesse de Ségur, I'm talking seriously, man to man, and I repeat: I have no sin within me, and that's something that can't be explained, that can't be debated, it's a mystery, period, and you'll never force me to go to confession, and if nobody wants to believe me, fuck him! It means nothing to me to rot away all alone in a corner till the end, I'm used to it. Anyway, what does confession actually give a person? Repenting for your sins will never change the past."

Suddenly he looked stupid and I watched him squeeze the goat's head that tops his cane to stifle his aggressive instincts in response to the slight obscenity that I'd dared to spit up, but he still had some cards up his sleeve.

"In a way, Frédéric, I can understand your anger and your outrage, but I don't wish you any harm, I give you my word as a friend. To tell the truth you're not, alas, the first young man I've seen lapse into anger, but I want you to understand that sickness, whatever the outcome, leads the sick person to salvation; and I would like it if by accepting faith, you agree to receive unction as a baptized member of the Church, because you were baptized by your parents who love you and who wanted nothing but good for you through that baptism, all the good in the world, don't ever forget that, and know that the Church, your Church, does not despair in the face of death, but wants to hold up for you the lamp of faith to guide your footsteps as you go towards the Almighty; and know too that you cannot forgive yourself for your own sins, only God can do that, God whose minister I am among men."

He put it well, but it left me cold.

"Now you listen to me, Mister Minister . . . If my baptism made my parents happy in the past, good for them, I wish them all the good in the world, but I'm grownup now and I'm the one who decides, and whether or not my parents love me doesn't change a thing of what's waiting for me or of what I can see now that I'm where I am. And I can see that I don't need anyone to help me pass away in the night."

At those words, Abbé Guillemette picked his nose and thought very hard, hard enough to give him cramps in the eyebrows, then he looked me in the whites of my eyes, genuinely sad.

"You seem to be thinking only of yourself, poor Frédéric, but it's not just your own little personal sin that matters, there is also sin in general, the sins of the world. As a young Christian, you must learn to carry with all others the weight of universal sin which causes all the woes of humankind, and if you refuse to put up with the repercussions of sin that remain after forgiveness, it is God's gift that you are refusing within yourself, and it's as if you wanted to adopt the point of view of God, which is reserved for God alone, and *that* is a sin, the one that we call the act of pride, which was actually the first sin in the world, the one that caused Adam to lose sanctity and immortality."

Yeah, so they say, but if he didn't want to lose his innocence with the first woman who came along, the first man could have just hanged himself from the tree of the knowledge of good and evil, and we'd be easy in our minds today.

"I hate to tell you this, Monsieur l'Abbé, but I have nothing to be ashamed of in the presence of the immortals, because I am as pure as the driven snow, according to my mother, who is also perfect, my mother who is better than the good Lord at forgiveness, and most of all, don't try to tell me that talking out loud and saying what we think are sins, because the true sin, the gravest sin in this world, was committed by God when he created man, and he's the one who should ask our forgiveness for all the harm he's done to humankind, he's the one who ought to fast during Lent and go to confession, the one who ought to flog himself in the street and ask to be crucified, and don't come telling me about the freedom of men, that's too easy, and anyway, I detest your freedom so much it makes me puke, because it's always the same ones who talk about it and believe it, it's the rich who ramble on and on, and anyway, deep down maybe there are only accidents, everywhere, all the time."

Poor Abbé Guillemette didn't say anything else but he was pondering seriously, and sighing as he rubbed his temples. After weeks of seeing me he must have started to think that he would have to save me against my will.

"I don't hate you, Monsieur l'Abbé, in fact I'm quite fond of you, because you do your job as best you can, but I find it sad to see you wearing yourself out for nothing, given that everyone sees me as lost—lost to science as well as to religion, and anyway you and I are strangers to one another. The difference between the two of us is that I never needed to feel hell burning beneath my feet to do good and I didn't need God's sword on the back of my neck to love humankind."

In the end, most likely somewhat worn-out from working in the void as if it were some barbaric country, maybe thinking that he'd come back and work on me one day soon when my suffering and distress became unbearable, the

Abbé of desperate causes asked me if I would at least grant him permission to pray for me in the silence of his chapel; but even that I didn't want; that's right, I refused him even that solitary pleasure. I may be hard-hearted, but no one's going to pray for me behind my back, no one, never. And before the Abbé started to push it, I explained my last wishes. What I want is for my remains to be pitched onto a campfire at the chalet, that the others watch me sizzle, and when it's over, to shovel my ashes into a little plastic boat and launch it onto Missisquoi Bay from the end of the municipal wharf in Venise-en-Québec. They could christen my little boat with a quart of beer, or with cream soda if they want, I couldn't care less, as long as someone's foot pushes me out to sea forever. And that's it, that's all I want; it's simple enough, I think. And if somebody gets the idea of blaring out my poems around the fire at marshmallow time, I want them introduced as the work of the poet Metastasio, and after that I want them to be burned. After the show, let them forget my flames and my smoke; and for God's sake, no mass a year later! and most of all, no posthumous tributes: I'm allergic to signs of gratitude, the saccharine of weaklings. Nobody's going to bestow honors that I don't like, and if they do it will be one huge fucking mess. I'm capable of worse, you know, I told the Abbé; I'm capable of being resurrected right in your face, of coming back to possess you with all the satans I've been host to since I was born.

There you go, it's on that discordant note that I bid you farewell, O good Abbé Guillemette. You've shown great concern for my happiness and I thank you for it, and besides, I really did like your myrrh-scented robes—less so your magic, your fierce kindness and your spells; and I will see you eternally in your chapel, wrapped snugly in your veils like a fat, white-fleshed baby, but honestly, I don't feel the need to be saved, given that I can't see what I would be saved from. After all, death isn't a vice: it's just a pastime like any other. Anyway, I'm so thin that I wouldn't know in what nook or cranny of my carcass to put my sins. Nothing goes into it any more, my very being is cramped inside my thinness and all I want to keep inside me is my rare virtues, which are my family jewels.

Yes, I will die naked and ignorant, without benefit of any religion, the way I was born, the way we no longer know how to die.

■

While I am getting my breath back after the visit from the limping Abbé whose skull glistens with vanity, I start thinking about my poor grandmother Émilia who spends her time scurrying around, in spite of the bunions that make her limp slightly, my wonderful grandmother who goes back and forth between Sainte-Rose, Laval, and Montreal, searching all over, deep inside the malls and the dustiest bookstores, for the unattainable works of Pietro Metastasio, the old Italian poet now found only in the dictionary. I told my grandmother not to worry about it, to keep looking and not give up hope, and that in the meantime, I absolutely wanted to read about death, anything at all, whatever she could find at the nearest bookstore; but all the same, time was running out and that it was my last wish, I'd never ask her for anything after that.

"Given that I don't really know if I'll make it till Christmas," I told her on the phone, "I was wondering if I could give my present early . . ."

And one morning, my grandmother Langlois showed up in my bachelor pad with a secret under her coat—another sizzling book that she held in her arthritis-gnarled fingers like a hot coal: a volume entitled *Universal Death*, which begins with a remark by one Viscount de Chateaubriand, whom I don't know. "Life without pain is the hiccup of a child." That hit me hard, a dagger straight to the heart, because it's so true, so cruelly true.

That book which I needed so badly and anticipated as if

I were parched, I keep carefully hidden under my pillow; I don't talk about it to anyone, though I open it whenever I can, whenever I feel that I have the strength to be intelligent enough to understand what I'm going to read, and I go through it as the days go by, my blankets pulled over my head to isolate me from the world, like a hermit in his cave, and it is in silence and solitude that I've learned that the first known graves are in Mesopotamia, where the deceased, who had some deer remains in his hands and burned shells of ostrich eggs on his chest, exiled himself into lands from which there's no return, into the House of Darkness and Dust. That impressed me a lot and I went on to Oceania, where children preserve their parents' fleshless skulls; to Jericho, where shells were screwed into the eyes of the dead; to central Europe and Siberia, where graves were protected by the scapulae of mammoths; and everywhere, bodies were sprinkled with ochre, which is the symbol of blood, adorned with ivory beads, with the teeth of blue foxes worn as pendants, with necklaces of squirrel vertebrae or sable jaws.

In Africa, the deceased must first pass through the mess of brown, soft, stinking rot before they attain the higher order of the ancestor's white, hard, clean skeleton. There, death is associated with speech and is not complete until the name is lost, so that a man is truly dead when there's no longer anyone to call him; they take care though to dampen the speech of the dead by pouring water into his mouth, given that a dead man with a dry throat could never speak to the living. And then there are some good deaths, such as dying of old age, surrounded by your friends and family, peacefully, in harmony with the ancestors; and bad deaths, impure deaths caused by crime, drowning, suicide; hence the man who is buried will share either the fate of seeds or that of pebbles.

And sometimes, still in Africa, you could observe the sacrifice of the Master of the Spear who had himself buried alive so as to surprise and humiliate death; for the Celts, the children of the deceased were often burned alive; for the Etruscans, it was a hook-nosed demon, Charon, Son of the Night, who finished off the dying; and for the Norse, the murder of Ymir is the cause of life and of the world and Ymir's flesh is the earth, his bones the rocks, his blood the sea, his hair the clouds, his skull the sky, and the beginning is the murder of the god, the apocalypse, the murder of the cosmos; finally, the Aztecs sacrificed human victims to Huitzilopochtli, god of War, the Hunt, and the Sun, and master of the world.

I also learned that in the Arctic, wandering souls are tracked down by shamans who must split in two in order to exorcise shelters by capturing souls between the sticks and the skin of their drums. And among the Inuit, a sick person like me has lost his soul, which has been stolen by a bear or has disappeared into the moon; and when he dies, the sick person returns to the dwelling of the Sovereign, at the bottom of the sea.

I also like Egypt, where Râ, the creator with fourteen bodies who had fourteen chances of being immortal, replaced chaos with order, and where it is Pharaoh, who comes from the Sun and from the falcon-headed god of the Horizon, who continues the work of Râ; where the sky is a celestial cow that suckles Pharaoh and is united with him, a bull who makes his mother pregnant, merely to renounce his sins to delete them from divine memory; where the soul of the departed receives the light of the sun in heaven, while in the tombs, the embalmed bodies live the lives of corpses that don't decay, protected by the jackal-headed god, Anubis.

But I think that of all the places where a man can die, I would have chosen India, where Parsis who have come from Persia deposit their dead at the summit of a tower of silence to which vultures come to devour them; or one of the countries of the Buddha, where each person dreams of dying removed from the false comfort of objects; or in the countries of the Tao, where the deceased goes back to the childhood of the world, to the initial perfection of Nothingness, the Void, the Great, the One, which is true peace, true rest.

There, in the East, life is a dream which people believe as long as they are asleep, but death is the Great Awakening; and the breathing of humans is not content with air, but searches for emanations from the sun, the moon, and the stars. Yes, Asia was just right for me and me for Asia; and I would have liked to see my ashes travel down a liquid sky full of flowers, in the Ganges spiced from the maceration of corpses stuffed with curry.

People laugh at Lao Tse but he said: "Block all openings, close all doors, you will not be worn down at the end of your life." But that was a joke, I think, a subtle way to sneer at wimps, and it's what I understand when I read and re-read that sentence—I understand that an accomplished man is a man worn down by his mission, but that the man who stays new is a coward who has refused to live in the real world that eats us up. I noticed this: philosophers always tell us more on a second reading, because at first they conceal themselves— the better to unveil themselves afterwards. Basically, philosophers are like certain diseases that force us to fight in order to stay alive.

I've also noticed that religions are all well and good, but that eventually, they nauseate you and wear you out.

◆

Sadly happy and none too sure of himself, wearing his Boston Bruins tuque pulled down to his ears and his coat zipper undone, my little saint Benoît takes one last confused look around the bleak room where he nearly departed this life in the bed next to the window. I can read in his eyes his impatience to escape from this place for dying, as well as his pain at betraying us—but go in peace, my purified friend: your glomerulonephritis is now behind you, along with a stream of bad memories where my eyes shine, and if I'm silently jealous of your healing, it's only human, because basically I'm happy for you, I give you my word as a brother who's been cursed. Be brave and take the hand of the freedom that's come to seek you out from the rest of us, and don't worry about your pals: we're older than our arteries and we read philosophers; we know that a free man can't live without ever betraying anyone. Yes, we know all that, we aren't schoolchildren, and we forgive you for your ability to be healed.

In the air are
butterflies and prophets;

in the water,
drowned men and treasures;
in the fire,
lovers and martyrs;
and in the earth,
gold, potatoes and men,
as well as,
overnight,
oneself.

Ultimately, it is Benoît who'll have been right: he will live, and his life will be made up of many deeds and few words, it will be a real life, the kind we dream about, quite the opposite of my own poor life, but he is leaving with a murmur of the heart, which is a kind of rip in your tunic, a dark murmur in his consciousness, a secret wound that may have been caused by human grief, who knows?

We are unable to say anything to one another to conclude our friendship, but the best move has always been to tear oneself away from one's old habits without thinking about it. I see Benoît gulp as if he's swallowed something the wrong way and I watch his eyelashes tremble, and just when I sense that he's about to articulate an everlasting farewell, he finds the courage to turn on his heels and erase himself from our lives, with the shadow of disease, like the ghost of a degenerate scarlet fever, hot on his heels.

I could be mad at Benoît for abruptly returning to paradise and abandoning me to my Hell, but I've never admired him more than at this fateful moment when I'm losing him, when he unceremoniously amputates me, and anyway I know that he's weighed down with some epistles from a new testament: he is taking with him the greatest secret of our lives, my letters from purgatory hidden between his two carefully folded pairs of pajamas in the bottom of his little pilgrim's suitcase. To protect them from indiscreet gazes, he slipped them into the Astérix and Tintin books I gave him. In a little over a year, which is the little I have left, my friend will mail those letters, he swore on the Godhead, and then I'll be resurrected as a paper Messiah with ink as my blood, to brush against the Earth one last time, like a comet, before I disappear into the galactic solitudes for good.

Ashen-faced, dragged along by his satisfied parents who don't realize how cruel their joy is, Benoît disappeared, taking one look behind him, a mute cry that hit me smack in the chest and tore me apart. I'm in my bed, still crushed by it, speechless, and when I finally collect my scattered wits, my first thought is that, later on, when Benoît has become a nephrologist filled with emotion, he'll come back to see this room where we met, room number nine, and I'll still be here, translucent as a peaceful apparition, lying in this same metal bed on casters, and Benoît will see himself in the next bed, dazed by the years that will have passed in the time of a sigh, and I wonder what will be left of me in that future perfect, in that memory whose advent I've already been warned of, where I feel as if I already am, because all that is tomorrow. I may be immobilized in the grey light of eternity, like in a photograph, or else Benoît will recall vaguely a few tiny movements, the way I nodded my head or twitched my eyelids or moved my mouth when I talked; the look I wore when I was watching the clouds slip across the window, or when I bit into an apple; when I swallowed my cyclophosphamide tablets on an empty stomach, or when my mother appeared at my bedside like the Blessed Virgin in Portugal.

Doctor Benoît Caron may hear again the far-off echo of my broken voice; will perhaps remember a poem born from my pen; a smile on my lips; my slippers on my scrawny feet; my foliated hip; the dark circles under my eyes; some innocuous words I'll have spoken. But all these little nothings saved from oblivion will be a hint of my perfume that will float in infinity, the trace of light that I'll have left in time, and that a sensibility will have perceived by chance.

And that's what I will be, what I am: no reason to rewrite the Pentateuch.

> *Happy is he who steps outside*
> *in the way we enter a church.*

And for Marilou, my Indian princess, my poor despairing little Rilou, what will I be but a hallucination that she will confuse with her shower of nightmares?

In the filthy light of an ordinary early morning, very early, at the hour when disgust with life comes up from the pit of your stomach, they transferred Marilou to another hospital, one on Mount Royal, perhaps to bring her a little closer to the Côte-des-Neiges cemetery, to get her used to the heights of her imminent death, and I knew nothing about it. I didn't see her leave and I don't know what has become of her, if she's doing well or badly, if a bone marrow donation has saved her life or if the devil's blood is still bubbling in her veins.

I didn't save any of her poems, but I held onto the memory of her face and her voice, and the last words that we said to one another on the day before her departure.

She had asked me: "Do you think that we have a soul and that the soul will survive after we die?"

And I replied: "I don't know, but I don't think so . . . You?"

"I think we do, but I wish I didn't."

She was very afraid of the soul, you see, as if it were some barbaric punishment, and the survival of the spirit seemed to her like a sentence to fall forever inside herself, towards nothingness, in the broken self, the kingdom of entrails where each of us dies all alone in eternity.

"The thought that there may be nothing after death is the only one that, to me, resembles anything like hope."

And those were the last words of Marilou Desjardins; after them, Marilou vanished as if I had dreamed her up, on the same wind that had dropped her into the dream of my life. She went so quickly that I didn't even have time to make a child with her. Because yes, I would have done it with her, in a hospital bed with our IV lines all tangled together, yes, I would have liked to make love at least once in my life and do it well, for a good reason and with the right girl; not to reproduce myself though, to reproduce *her*, to bring more Marilou Desjardins into the world, to create other beauties like her for those who stay behind or those yet to come, to surprise and humiliate death; and together, we would have lost our virginities, but it's too late to do that well: I know I won't see her again, I can sense it, and I no longer have any friends.

The days go by and nothing stays behind,
not even the brightness of a thought;
and the days go badly
and turn to night;
and the nights combine their waters
in whirlpools
where my reflection is lost
in spirals among the stars.

My dreams have changed for the worse and my nights are starting to resemble a loop of little comas. I have no more future before me, I barely have a present pending, which is a weight on my heart, and the gazes in my sleep are all turned towards the past. I no longer read very much but I see my yesterdays again, a tangled heap in the darkness, all the old days I've lived that have the dignity of memories, and every wakening is a jolt, a falling into horror for me who wants to sleep, to sleep, to sleep some more, to drown myself in the night.

What's most heartbreaking is that I can see everything, and see it too well, all the way to some forbidden things that burn my eyes, and down my cheeks fall tears of fire, the blood of the beings in my life.

The Sun bathes in its vomit,
the Earth swirls in its neurosis
and beneath an orgy of stars shines the Moon,
placenta of humankind,
and on my blue planet,
on terra firma,
life rushes on
like a lady in the rain.

It's crazy, but a nurse told me not to give up hope because you never know, there still could be a miracle, seeing as how I'm in room number nine, yes, nine, which as it happens is the miracle number because its square root is the Trinity. She told me all that while she was washing my face and I was afraid it would leave its imprint on her washcloth like what happened on Veronica's veil.

Poor aunties. They're incredibly nice to us, that's not the problem, but I often wonder where they get their weird ideas. They think that when you close your eyes for good, the air is filled with angels but I, who don't live in their world, do not intend to die in their hereafter. I will die in my own, where there will be nothing, where we'll be at ease. The world may be what we want it to be; and maybe the other world too. Which would be fine with me.

That's it, my batteries are dead, I mean my transistor batteries, but I'll have had time to learn that the Shroud of Turin is a fake, that it's only seven hundred years old. Word has been quietly making the rounds of all the hospital corridors, but most people turn a deaf ear: their faith is so shaky that it wouldn't survive such a poor faded image; and from where I am I can hear my little saint Benoît preaching to them like a curé, raging at their sluggishness. "You ought to believe in the Invisible instead of hanging on to such childishness!" That's what Benoît would have told them, it seems to me, but life goes on at its own little pace, without turning around to contemplate its ruins, without even meditating on its illusions, and this afternoon we'll celebrate my memory in advance, and it will be one of those macabre parties that I dread so much, that are too reminiscent of the religions of the world: the feast of death. It's because my whole family is coming to see me, and my heart is beating fast and painfully. Soon they will turn the corner at the end of the corridor and we'll see them coming towards me under the fluorescent light, walking bags of presents. They'll knock on the door discreetly and, out of breath, stick their heads in the doorway to see if my companions in misfortune and I are still among the living. They will try to hide their relief at finding me alive in my bed and they'll smile when they see me raise my eyebrows, then they'll approach, dragging behind them a long tail of cold air, with the wild smell of winter mixed in with their hair.

Mama will have fussed with her appearance and I can already see her moist eyes shining in the light. I can also make out her gold earrings with the little coral stones; her fuchsia scarf that will hide her sinewy neck that she's never liked; her long, waxy, be-ringed fingers; and already it seems to me that her light spicy perfume is driving away the sickening smell of drugs.

Allowing himself to drive blindly in this uncaring world, Papa will be clinging to Mama's arm, all bound up in his Sunday clothes but with a carefully knotted tie, somewhat thinner, long-faced, with dark circles under his eyes and his hair tamed, but out of breath, his gaze darkened by a vague nausea. He'll say hello to me very softly, with a movement of his head, then my frightened sister and brother will drag their feet, not far behind, mouths open and noses running.

With a deceptively cheerful look, they'll greet my comrades who are also expecting visitors, then they'll pile their coats awkwardly on my wheelchair. A tuque, a mitten will land on the floor. Charlotte will kiss me while Bruno will look me in the eyes, not moving, paralyzed with fear at the foot of the bed. My parents will sit on the edge of the mattress, cautiously so they won't break me, and the snow from outside will melt under their salt-stained boots, forming puddles of dirty water all around my bed.

While Charlotte helps me unwrap my presents, mama will gently rub my feet and papa will smooth my dishevelled hair with his cold damp hand. We'll talk about the chalet buried in snow up to the roof; about Rivière aux Brochets that streams, lean and murmuring, under its crust of ice; and about the frozen Mississquoi Bay that seems to be thinking while it waits for me down there beneath the transparent winter sky.

They'll give me the latest news about my hockey team, the Sainte-Philomène Titans, who are winning without me in the net; about my dog, Voyou, who sleeps at the foot of my empty bed and looks for me inside all the closets; about my classmates who've made me a huge get-well card. Then they'll touch my face, my hands, very delicately as if I were a crystal vase. They will want me to feel precious, but I'll get lost in all their arms, lonely and as useless as a jewel.

It is then that a voice will be heard in my head, a malevolent voice from deep inside me, that will make me look up at my mother.

I will think: "Mama, I beg you, keep your precious tears for your other son, I'm not worth it, I'm not the one you expected or the one that you think you will miss. You think that you know me because you conceived me, bore me, gave birth to me, and fed me at your breast, but you don't know the poor quality of your milk. You see, the archangels betrayed you, O Mother: I'm rotten inside, it's written in the gospels, and my bones are decayed. Jesus loves me on account of my sins, as if they were the only thing of value about me; but I'm not a sinner, and I feel lost and defiled by Jesus. The Bible threatens me with death but I've never committed the evil I'm accused of, the evil we see everywhere. All I've done was to be born, to open my eyes to the light, and all I wanted was to live with the small amount I'd received from the stars. If Jesus hadn't known how to multiply the loaves and fishes, he'd have stolen them, the way I stole an apple from the supermarket one day when I was hungry. I'm no less perfect than Christ; just less powerful. Does that make me a bird of ill omen? Poor Mama, I don't want you to cry, I want you to save your tears for when Voyou is run over by a drunk driver, because on that day you'll have to cry for two, you'll have to cry for me who will no longer have eyes to do it himself."

After that, I'll look at my father and think: "Papa, I've never known who that strange creature is who's been hidden deep inside me forever, who was there before me, before I was born. I've always been very afraid of that dark power buried in my head, afraid of what might come from it; and I know today that I was right to have chattering teeth. I am someone whom I've never seen anywhere, whom I hope I'll never see again. The saddest thing is that I come from you, who didn't deserve this, but I'm abandoning you here, I won't go any further in your religion, I don't want to operate inside your hope: I would be liable to soil it badly. That's because a madman is talking through my mouth, but rather than slit his throat as a good son ought to do, I listen to him and I don't believe that he's wrong. Papa, I look at you the way I've looked at the beautiful holy images of my childhood: I love you, but from a distance, and I'd never have wanted to live your life. I move farther away every day, step by step; I move away from you, from mama and all the others, so far that the ties between us break, and I can now see better what we really are: beings of mist who cluster together to form a small, cautious people lost in advance. Sometimes I actually think that you begot me out of jealousy and don't even know it, but I forgive you. The fact remains that unconsciously, you envied me for not being alive, not existing, not suffering in the world; so one night you made mama pregnant and the spark of my life burst forth. You conceived me out of revenge and that revenge has been of some use: today when you are no longer alone as you tremble in the face of death, the illusion of numbers makes you think that you have one small chance of escaping it. That's something you wanted to make me see because others before you had wanted you to see it, and that pain was something you had to share, as Christians do when they break bread, and only then does the pain becomes bearable; but it doesn't matter, dear Papa, no, it doesn't matter at all, it's only human, and you won't have been the first man to look to others for his salvation. Just think, it was Saint Joseph himself who built the cross for his son, because that is the true profession of all fathers, the hidden legacy of man that is lost in the mists of time."

Then I will look at Charlotte and think: "Dear little sister, you've grown up behind my back without my seeing it, and here you are further away than a stranger. You are a hand puppet who moves in front of cardboard sets and I don't know the names of the winds that blow inside you and bring you to life. I wish I could have known you better, and maybe one day we'll have things to tell one another, but I'm already a mute silhouette who is walking away in the night, stooping in the rain, head filled with different expressions of nostalgia, of which you are the youngest."

Finally, I will look at Bruno and think: "O my brother, I

know that you're jealous of me, that you would like to suffer more than I do. In your sweetest dreams you see yourself gravely ill, even dying, and all the girls are crying at your bedside and admiring your ordeal, but deep down you're a softy, like everybody else: you're too cowardly to pray for God to send you a real cancer. You're just a fucking little weakling, the kind that can be seen at every street corner, a poor birdbrain: you can't even imagine what it's like to open your eyes in the morning with the old reflex for happiness still inside you, then suddenly remember that you're terminally ill. May Heaven protect you from that knowledge, O kid brother. I hope that you'll be thankful to your lucky star when you pack it in as an old man, adrift in an institutional bed as vast and frigid as an ice floe, between government sheets; and remember to spare a thought for me before you give up the ghost; for me who'll have been dead for ages; me, the hero you envied during your whole life. But don't worry too much about how mean-spirited I could be, poor Bruno: if I pierce you so thoroughly with my fiery gaze, it's because your blood and mine were once mixed, because your lifeline extends into my hand, because my heart is crawling with the same gnawing worms: I have all your despicable and shameful behavior too; and all the evil things that I've just said about you, I've found deep inside myself."

My family are poor innocents and I feel a painful pity for them, because they don't know that the world of appearances can mislead them so easily. If they love me, it's not because I am the boy I am, but because I'm of the same blood. If they're here at my bedside, it's not because I am dying but because a particle of themselves is. If I did not embody that familiar light they think they recognize within themselves, they wouldn't give a damn about me, just as they don't give a damn about any other dying person; and if they were Bélangers or Gravels or Tremblays they'd avoid hospitals, yet I would still be the same boy, I'd be myself, Frédéric Langlois, from the parish of Sainte-Philomène, born on the fourth of March in the Miséricorde Hospital, afflicted with the same rotten hip and the same cancer of the soul.

It's crazy, but that story makes me as delirious as the prophets and I'm more surprised than anyone: yes, it's my turn to say with a straight face that you have to love the whole world—murderers, lepers, rapists, atheists, junkies, Nazis, prostitutes . . . Either that or not love anyone, or else what you have in the belly is a humankind that's neither flesh nor fowl; it's half a sun that sheds insufficient light on men who are lost, half a firmament that's riddled with metastases.

It's as simple as ABC: you forgive absolutely everything or absolutely nothing. Both roads are possible and equally valid, but if you decide to forgive you have to understand that it's a spiral, the spiral of forgiveness. Pure, true love is light years away from reason, because everyone is someone else as well, me most of all: I've never been the little angel people thought. I had promised to be a worthy man till the end, but I've fallen flat and I shall be ashamed for all eternity; I am a mutant with a heart no bigger than a wild strawberry and I deserve all the crap that lands on me. I have pains that radiate to my guts like the rays of a blazing sun; I can feel that my hip is crumbling, that my chalky bones are disintegrating, that the wind is taking the dust that is me into the darkness.

Okay, that's it, that's it, it's happened, it's happening to me, and already my knees are sagging under the weight of my native anguish that is added to all the anguish I've been given for my own good, that makes my hair fall out and my gums bleed, before my teeth fall out tomorrow. What's worst is that the tragedy of loss brings glory to feeble souls: you just have to be a tormented man, condemned to seek a meaning for his life amid chaos, to moan because you don't understand what's going on, and you'll always find naïve girls to praise these brief thoughts, which are as immature as the nightmares of a child who can't stop being aware of existence, and to follow his reasoning all the way to the end of infinity.

Yes, women are too gentle, too pure, too good for this world without pity; they allow us to have a glimpse of the paradise that the universe could have been and that rips out the heart of men who are going to die; as for me though, my mind is made up: I push away both love and life and that rejection is my morphine; even if God should suddenly appear to me like a last-minute peek-a-boo to snatch me from my grave, I would refuse with my last burst of strength his scattering of miracles. Yes, I swear on the heads and the blood of the children of Bangladesh, I cross my heart: if God should get involved and come to save me against my will, I'd kill myself in front of him to show him the meaning of courage and contempt; I'd slash my wrists, I'd hang myself in the cellar, I'd blow my brains out or, even better, I would bury myself alive like an African Master of the Spear. Fear of suffering doesn't rule out the fact that sometimes a person has to die young as a matter of principle, and such a superhuman sacrifice is no longer beyond my strength: anyway, I've had enough of visionaries who get drunk on miracles here and remarkable feats there—the miracle of drawing all one's happiness from the passing moment; the remarkable feat of getting used to every form of disgust and to live a happy life in spite of human misery—and their tears of joy disgust me; but soon I'll be set free, because I have chosen my destiny: it will be that of men who've been abandoned to their fate since the dawn of time.

I've heard that somewhere in the Bible, God regrets having made man on Earth, and that his heart is filled with misgivings, but I'll never read that with my own eyes. It's too late: I've already asked my grandmother Émilia to administer extreme unction with her scent of daffodils or carnations, and I told her to bring her beautiful rosary of the dead, the one whose hollow beads are filled with earth from the catacombs of Rome—that magic rosary must work marvellously well and I'm in the mood to hear some Hail Mary's recited by my grandmother whose voice is the music of my childhood. While I wait I'll get good and drunk on chokecherry eau-de-vie: that would be good for me, it would numb my brains a little, like the wine mixed with myrrh in the Gospels, and I would lift my chalice of blood to the solitude of the night; to the sorrow of those who don't believe in anything and who have come into the world to lose everything; to the forces that surpass me and of which I am the prey; but I'd drink badly, it's inevitable: my people weren't born in the vines, they're shovellers of clouds and they guzzle snow. The best thing is that, with a little luck, I may die on December 25, like a little Antichrist. From the depths of my hell I'll be able at last to curse this world of

lethargic poets who, as they search for prizes, apply themselves to making poems from the death and suffering of others and, frankly, that deserves one last cruddy poem.

> *I depart without believing,*
> *I am extinguished*
> *without having flamed,*
> *like a stick of incense*
> *that reeks of*
> *the mass for the dead.*

Again and again, I repeat those last desperate lines, because
the Grim Reaper isn't unionized; she doesn't work shifts and
she can descend from heaven when it strikes her fancy. It's
different from the Santa Clauses in their helicopters. And it's
not like the poor pawns in rags at Christmastime, characters
in living crèches who freeze their feet in the snow outside
churches for an audience of infantile lunatics. In any event,
if God really wants to exist for the humans to come, I
strongly advise him to turn up astride a fine ray of sunshine,
one of those that dazzle in the light of an adoration; otherwise, his ghost-skin wouldn't be worth much to the head-
hunters. As far as his life is concerned, I've had a hell of a
good taste of it, and I'm fading away with a grimace, but

then again, maybe I'll weep with joy when I plunge into the darkness of the grave. Who knows? We know so little about ourselves that we must always anticipate the worst.

It's crazy, but I wonder why we have such a great need for good and evil in order to live on this earth. And why can awe not touch grace until we've given up the ghost? What does it have to lose, that snobby grace that can't bring happiness to living people? But I console myself with the thought that evil isn't what we think it is: evil is the vicious thought that a man can't save himself on his own, but that a slug of rotgut will take care of it.

Ah! That's it, that's it, eureka! I think I've finally found my last words, the real thing!

Lightning has struck my pen and here is its child:

> *We die the way we emigrate,*
> *dreaming of peace and riches,*
> *our hearts as big as a native land.*

Yes, that's it exactly, I've finally captured the sphinx of my nights, that's exactly what I want people to remember about me. What the hell! At last, at last! When I die I'll be off to a good start for becoming a legend. Finally, my whole life will have been spent solely to end up with those few words that will be my last human traces in the snow, and I thank the stars for permitting me to breath until now. It's not much, that's certain, it's the Himalaya giving birth to a guinea pig, but it is my essence; it's the poisoned gift that I leave in my little furrow, to those who have eyes to see and a heart to break. My poetry will have been a Sodom and Gomorrah, and the world, a Lot's wife; and I'll have been a drunkard's promise, a rainy summer, a pedigree of a dog killed in the traffic, a false pregnancy, a miscarriage. To the very end, I'll have bitten the hand that fed me, because poetry doesn't save poets from any ills, it walls them up, alive, inside everything that they've always known. I understand, but I'm getting tired. There's a needle planted in my arm and through it flows into my veins, drop by drop, truth serum or snake venom, and I will have killed myself by saying everything that I really thought. Yes, I've said so many true things this last while that I've lost all my vital strength, committed suicide off the planet Earth, far away, light years from men, from women, from my people who are suffering because they no longer recognize me, I'm dribbling malice like a cholera, but I have no desire whatsoever to exchange my heart of stone for a medal for bravery. In any event, it's stupid to laugh and I'm sorry I laughed: we always collapse in the end, and here I am with heavy eyelids, shivering from weakness; I'm sick to my stomach and dizzy; and anyway, just now when I drank some water, I left something like the trace of a woman's kiss on the edge of my glass, but it isn't lipstick, no, it's something else, something much more serious: it's the skin of my bleeding mouth that's coming loose in strips that stick to everything. They are farewell kisses that I'm giving to the world, kisses of death, and I'm all unwound: this is a very bad day that is launching the beginning of the end.

I just have to pick up my doodads, collect my belongings, pack up the kids, turn off the water and the electricity, close the blinds (and then evaporate into nature, slamming the parenthesis).

The poet Metastasio has gone to bed.

God hate his soul. Anyway, fuck.